E R S

The two fight, ea
She fights against her t
They fight on, nev

was gradually whittled down. Eventually, they were ordered to go on a long-term Special Reconnaissance mission—a hopeless pursuit that effectively meant their execution.

With tears in her eyes, Lena supported the squadron as they made their way over the horizon. In that same battle, Shin fulfilled his long-awaited desire by gunning down his older brother, Rei, whose consciousness had been assimilated by the Legion.

Exchanging their final good-byes over the Para-RAID, Lena bid farewell to her days with Shin and the others...

EIGHTY-SIX
STORY

ILLUSTRATION BY SHIRABII   MECHANICAL DESIGN BY I-IV

Anju

A surviving memb
of the Spearhead
squadron. A girl w
appears graceful at
glance but is as ruth
on the field of batt
as any of her mal
companions. Perso
Name: Snow Witc

Raiden

The Spearhead
squadron's vice captain.
Shin's right-hand
man, who is always
supporting him. Personal
Name: Wehrwolf.

The word on everyone's lips was "Why?"

They couldn't know that for *them*, asking why is an insult.

For *they* are...the Eighty-Six.

—FREDERICA ROSENFORT, *RECOLLECTIONS OF THE BATTLEFIELD*

86—EIGHTY-SIX

Vol. 2

ASATO ASATO

Translation by Roman Lempert
Cover art by Shirabii

This book is a work of fiction. Names, characters, places, and incidents are the product of the author's imagination or are used fictitiously. Any resemblance to actual events, locales, or persons, living or dead, is coincidental.

86—Eighty-Six—Ep. 2
©ASATO ASATO 2017
First published in Japan in 2017 by KADOKAWA CORPORATION, Tokyo.
English translation rights arranged with KADOKAWA CORPORATION, Tokyo,
through TUTTLE-MORI AGENCY, INC., Tokyo.

English translation © 2019 by Yen Press, LLC

Yen On
150 West 30th Street, 19th Floor
New York, NY 10001

Visit us at yenpress.com

facebook.com/yenpress
twitter.com/yenpress

yenpress.tumblr.com
instagram.com/yenpress

First Yen On Edition: July 2019

Yen On is an imprint of Yen Press, LLC.
The Yen On name and logo are trademarks of Yen Press, LLC.

The publisher is not responsible for websites (or their content) that are not owned by the publisher

Library of Congress Cataloging-in-Publication Data
Names: Asato, Asato, author. | Shirabii, illustrator. | Lempert, Roman, translator.
Title: 86—eighty-six / Asato Asato ; illustration by Shirabii ; translation by Roman Lempert.
Other titles: 86—eighty-six. English
Description: First Yen On edition. | New York, NY : Yen On, 2019–
Identifiers: LCCN 2018058199 | ISBN 9781975303129 (v. 1 : pbk.) | ISBN 9781975303143 (v. 2 : pbk.)
Subjects: CYAC: Science fiction.
Classification: LCC PZ7.1.A79 .A18 2019 | DDC [Fic]—dc23
LC record available at https://lccn.loc.gov/2018058199

ISBNs: 978-1-9753-0314-3 (paperback)
978-1-9753-0315-0 (ebook)

5 7 9 10 8 6

TPA

Printed in South Korea

HER MAJESTY IS NOT ON THE BATTLEFIELD

"You again, *Lieutenant* Vladilena Milizé?"

Regarding Lena with a glance as she entered the office, the commanding officer seated behind the desk grimaced. His uniform was worn out, and his chin was covered in stubble. This officer, who almost seemed out of place in these times of peace, lowered his gaze from Lena, who stood perfectly at ease before him.

She wore an immaculate, starched black uniform, and her silver hair flowed like silk, with the exception of one section, which she had dyed red. She had adopted this look six months ago, when the Spearhead squadron—a squadron of Eighty-Six—had been sent to the battlefield on a suicide mission. As they were not allowed to return, their only option was to advance into enemy territory until they were killed in action.

Ever since, she had worn black to mourn them and dyed a portion of her hair red to signify their shed blood. Although it had been in clear violation of her orders, she had launched covering fire for them and been demoted a single rank as punishment. She would likely never be able to rise beyond the rank of lieutenant.

"Unauthorized firing of an interception cannon. Supplying your troops with an unregistered warhead and other supplies, as well as giving direct commands to other squadrons. Please refrain from creating more unnecessary trouble and paperwork over a bunch of Eighty-Six,

Lieutenant. Do you have any idea how many complaints I've received about you from transports and supplies?"

"You wouldn't be getting any complaints if my requests had been approved, Lieutenant Colonel. If those complaints truly bother you so much, then feel free to gripe about them as much as you want, but I honestly could not care less."

A crease formed under one of the lieutenant colonel's eyes, which had become heavy lidded due to his severe alcoholism.

"Watch your mouth, young lady. A lieutenant like you should know her place."

Lena gave a thin, cold smile. He tried to pressure her with his rank and nothing else, only proving he didn't have the nerve to actually punish her in any way. Lena's squadron boasted the highest Legion-extermination rate on the eastern front. And the achievements of one's subordinates translated directly into the achievements of their commanding officer.

Since the ground forces had been decimated at the opening stages of the war, this man, who had managed to claw his way up to the rank of lieutenant colonel, desired to climb ever higher. To him, Lena and her achievements were like a hen that lays golden eggs.

So long as her *pranks* didn't go too far, he would defend her no matter what.

"I'll be taking my leave, Lieutenant Colonel."

She gave an elegant salute.

As she walked down a corridor of the palace that served as the military's headquarters—a luxurious building, even for the first ward, that was rich with beautiful, antiquated architecture—she could hear the whispers of disdain and see the scornful glares all around her.

There she is, the fool who threw away the rank of major and any hope of promotion to the higher echelons, all for a bunch of Eighty-Six. A princess who can't even distinguish people from livestock. An idiot who, even though the Legion will all stop functioning in a year, danced to the tune of the pigs' lies when they said they had to prepare for the war to last longer. Everyone knows it's going to end soon.

*The cruel, merciless, inhumane Bloodstained Queen, Bloody Reina,
who forces the filthy stains to fight to the death even though they're already
on the verge of extinction.*

Ridiculous.

The RAID Device on Lena's neck activated, and she stopped in her
tracks. Clicking the heels of her boots, she continued walking down the
beautiful wooden hallway with a quicker gait.

"Can you hear me, Handler One?"

"Cyclops. More Legion? What's the situation?"

The rough voice that spoke to her through the Para-RAID belonged
to Captain Shiden Iida, Personal Name: Cyclops. The squadron Cyclops
led under Lena's commanded came to be known as the Queen's Knights.

Ever since the incident with the Spearhead squadron, Lena had
taken to asking the Processors for their names on the first day she took
up a new post. However, she never referred to them by anything but
their Personal Names. She couldn't, because once before, she'd called her
Processors by their real names with the intent of treating them as equals.
But in the end, she couldn't save them from the fate of dying as drones,
with their graves unmarked and their names forgotten.

**"They made it all the way into point 112 in the old high-speed transit
terminal. It's our bad; the radar failed on us, and we noticed them too late…
This fight's gonna be hard on the newbies."**

Lena clicked her tongue bitterly. Yes, it was bound to be difficult.
A single mistake on the battlefield with zero casualties could lead to
countless lost lives.

"Head to point 062 and lure them in with a detached force. That
point should be in range of the other interception cannons. The road
should be dense with private residences, so it should put the Juggernaut's
smaller fuselage at an advantage."

Cyclops laughed loudly.

**"You're firing this close to the base? If you miss, forget this Sector—
you might end up hitting your Republic's minefield."**

"But if we're to survive this, that's the optimal bombardment site."

Hearing that flat, resolute statement, Cyclops laughed again.

Survive. They, the Eighty-Six, and Lena, in the Republic, beset on all sides by the Legion.

Survive, she'd said.

For the sake of the ones who believed she would fight and live on.

"Roger that, Your Majesty... I'll contact you again once we're in position. Let me know if you learn anything new."

The Para-RAID cut off, and Lena hastened her stride, heading for the control room, only to pause a moment later when something outside the window caught her attention. The paved streets of the Republic of San Magnolia, populated only by silver-haired, silver-eyed Alba. The Republic's five-hued flag, which stood for freedom, equality, brotherhood, justice, and nobility and bore the image of Saint Magnolia, the saint of the revolution, fluttered under a dim-blue spring sky.

Soon, the season in which she'd made first contact with the Spearhead squadron would come again. They, who saw reaching their final destination as their vision of freedom, who saw fighting to the bitter end as their pride, who left while laughing happily. They, who would never return.

Where were they now? In a field of blooming spring flowers, perhaps?

She prayed that, at the very least, they would be allowed to rest in peace.

86

[EIGHTY-
SIX]

Life, land, and legacy.
All reduced to a number.

2
RUN THROUGH THE BATTLEFRONT (START)

ASATO ASATO

ILLUSTRATION: Shirabii

MECHANICAL DESIGN: I-IV

86

[EIGHTY- SIX]

The word on everyone's lips was "Why?"
They couldn't know that for *them*,
asking why is an insult.

86
⌈ EIGHTY-
SIX ⌋

CHAPTER 1

RIDE OF THE VALKYRIES

The skies on the front lines were concealed behind thin clouds of Eintagsfliege, their eerily serene silver spreading as far as the eye could see.

"There's another force of Löwe coming your way, estimated to be a battalion-size group...! We've got a platoon heading our way, too!"

The squadron's wireless radios were abuzz with frantic status updates. The fighting so far had claimed 30 percent of their forces, and the news of the encroaching Löwe spelled death for the 12th Company of the 141st Regiment of the Federal Republic of Giad's 177th Armored Division, which had only been pushed farther back with every passing moment.

"Forty-five seconds until contact! Oh, God...!"

"Tch... There's more of 'em coming...?!"

Eugene, the violent prodigy of combat maneuverability, groaned from the tandem cockpit of his Vánagandr. He had the silver hair and eyes of a pureblood Celena. Though he wore glasses, his face was still youthful for a seventeen-year-old.

Against the Federacy, the Legion employed a ruthless tactic—one unit would detach itself from combat and sneak off to summon reinforcements. Before long, that one would become many, and the newly formed horde would then rejoin the fray. The Federal Republic of Giad's

third-generation Feldreß Vánagandr was able to rival the Löwe for domi-
nance over ground warfare. Inferior units simply wouldn't stand a chance.
"Shit, what is the artillery brigade doing?!
Where was the cover fire?!"

He could hear the company commander, who sat in the back seat as
the vehicle's gunner, swear bitterly over the radio. Due to the heavy stride
of the eight-legged Vánagandr, the reverberations of its tank turret, and
·the screeching of its energy packs, it was impossible to hear anything or
hold a conversation within the cockpit, even from a short distance.

The commander, of course, was perfectly aware of this. Bathed in
the darkness created by ceaseless deployment of the Eintagsfliege, his
radar and sensors were dead, and it was impossible to pinpoint the enemy's location with eyesight alone. Battles against the Legion always
began as one-sided onslaughts.

Equipped with cracked reinforced-armor exoskeletons and 12.8 mm
heavy machine guns, armored infantry faced off against the Dragoon-type
Grauwolf but only ended up getting crushed along with the trenches
they inhabited. Meanwhile, their supporting unit, a fellow Vánagandr,
was equipped with thick composite armor and a 120 mm barrel cannon
that was unmatched in strength. But the resulting lack of mobility led to
it being crushed as well.

The Legion were machines designed for slaughter, and human
reflexes couldn't stand up to their reaction speed. The Vánagandr was
especially weak when it came to acceleration; even if in terms of inherent
cruising speed, it could match the Legion's forces, when it came to com-
prehensive motion capabilities like accelerating, braking, or swiveling, it
fell fatally behind.

"Don't flinch! Even if you dodge them, it's not
like they're gonna let you run!"
"Come at me, you shitty pieces of scrap metal!
It'll be my fucking honor to shield my comrades, you hear me?!"
"God dammit, like hell I'm dying here! I refuse
to be taken...!"

FRIENDLY UNIT

The Federal Republic of Giad's Primary Offensive Feldreß

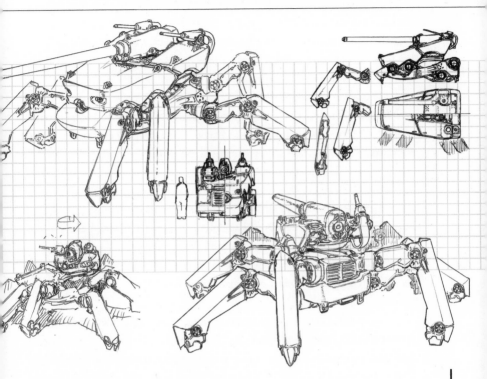

M4A3 Vánagandr

[SPECS]

Manufacturer: Felswinzel Military Industries
Total Length: 6.5 m / Height: 2.9 m

[ARMAMENTS]

120 mm Smoothbore Turret ×1
12.7 mm Heavy Machine Gun ×2

Note: Features a tandem cockpit, with one pilot serving as the driver and the other serving as gunner and unit captain.

A third-generation Feldreß mobilized as the Federacy's primary offensive force. Its powerful turret and thick armor allow it to easily overpower the Ameise and Grauwolf, and its defensive prowess keeps its pilots safe and sound. However, as its specs are slightly lower than the Löwe, which serves as the Legion's primary force, it maintains the front lines with coordinated attacks via control and human-wave tactics.

The infantrymen tried to shrug off their impending deaths, pelting the mechanical demons that approached them with jeers and bullets as nightmare-inducing screams haunted the radio waves. Eugene gritted his teeth as the voices, which had already come to grips with their fates even as they fought, echoed in his ears.

Beeeep. Their request for reinforcements, which they had been broadcasting since the beginning of the battle, had finally been answered, as signaled by a beep. And that's when it happened.

Several shells cruised through the air, cutting through the pale-blue moonlight and the darkness of night as if it were thin gauze. They landed on the upper section of the defensive Legion's line with startling accuracy, some bursting and others unleashing showers of smaller explosives onto them. The bombardment was concentrated perfectly, missing the armored infantry's fan formation and landing only on the Legion that lay deeper within.

The bombardment was nothing short of a superhuman feat. The thinly armored Scout types—Ameise—had been collectively silenced. The Grauwolf were purged by a barrage of rockets fired at their rear. The lightweight Legion may have had their combat capabilities reduced, but the Tank-type Löwe swerved their cannon turrets, unscathed…until they crumpled to the ground a moment later, having taken armor-piercing rounds to their flanks.

And as the deafening roars of the Löwe's consecutive cannon fire and their constant clouds of dust and rumbles fell silent, Eugene could finally hear it from afar, echoing like distant thunder. With an initial velocity of 1,600 meters per second, which far exceeded the speed of sound, the cannon's shot made an impact long before it could be heard. The impact was followed by the sharp, heavy, distinctive sound of metal plates banging against one another.

"An 88 mm…?!"

"Ugh, don't tell me it's…!"

It lunged at the Legion through the darkened sky like a jumping spider ravenously plucking insects from the ground. Landing on top of a Löwe at the center of the enemy formation, it drove the four electromagnetic pile drivers in its legs into the Löwe's back. The Löwe spasmed and twitched violently.

It had four nimble jointed legs and pure-white armor, the color of polished bone. Its two grappling arms, each equipped with a pair of high-frequency blades and a wire anchor, were currently folded up like a spider's chelicerae, and on its back was a gun mount arm supporting an 88 mm smoothbore gun. The 57 mm pile drivers on the tips of each of its four legs gleamed a brilliant shade of silver.

The machine was blessed with a cold, ferocious beauty befitting the name Valkyrie, but simultaneously, it also evoked the terrifying image of a skeletal corpse prowling the battlefield in search of its lost head.

"A Reginleif…"

The groan that leaked from the onboard wireless comm sounded less like something one might say in the face of an ally that came to provide backup and more like an utterance of fear in the face of an enemy.

The XM2 Reginleif. It was the polar opposite of the Vánagandr, which had heavy composite armor that stood for absolute defensive capabilities and a 120 mm cannon that encompassed maximum penetrating force. The Reginleif's explosive output stood in direct opposition to its weight, and its powerful and highly efficient linear actuators granted this late third-generation Feldreß high mobility.

For having emphasized maneuverability, the Reginleif sacrificed defense and firepower, and its hypermobility even damaged its passengers' bodies. It was a third-generation high-mobility combat aircraft designed by what was seemingly sheer madness. It was based off "their" machines: the diabolical drones created by the Republic on the other side of the Legion-infested territories.

The Legion lacked all traces of life and compassion and felt no sorrow for their fallen comrades. They did not fear death. The Löwe swiftly shifted their primary objective, preparing to shoot down the Reginleif, which had been caught in the wreckage of a downed consort unit.

Leaping out of harm's way at the very last second, the Reginleif fired at a stranded Löwe that ran aground a moment later. Its turret, weighing several tons, was blown off as its own ammunition exploded, soaring high into the air. The combat unit went up in an ostentatious ball of flames, a precaution to protect sensitive data from enemy hands.

The Reginleif rushed on, darting through flames of red and black, as well as a lethal rain of metal debris. Closing the fifty-meter gap between the Tank types within moments, it performed a short-range leap toward a Löwe just as it rotated its turret, spraying the Löwe's vulnerable flank with armor-piercing rounds from its 88 mm cannon as they intersected. Without pause, it cut down a group of Grauwolf that charged at it with its high-frequency blades before leaping to single-handedly engage the next Löwe.

Yes, single-handedly.

It was only one unit, but that one unit alone decimated a largely intact company of augmented, armored Legion. Its high-frequency blade screeched, its pile drivers discharged purple bolts of electricity, and its 88 mm cannon shook the battlefield with its roars, reducing the infernal hunks of iron to mere scrap metal.

This feat was not a testament to the machine's capabilities. Rather, the praise belongs to its pilots—once known as Processors when they manned the cruelly named drones—and their skills, which made all the difference.

The loss-exchange ratio between the Reginleif and the Löwe wasn't significantly higher than that of the Vánagandr and the Löwe, and the casualty rate of the Reginleif was, in fact, higher. In reality, when a test unit of Reginleifs was deployed during its trial stages, all but one company were cornered into annihilation—and that same company, led by *them*, wiped out the enemy force in its entirety.

The berserk soldiers who were rescued from the depths of hell by the Federacy walked right back into that hell of their own free will. *They* didn't fear going into battle with the Legion, didn't flinch in the face of the deaths that awaited them. Shunning armor, they rode the Reginleifs, which made light of the lives of their pilots, and hunted the Legion down with an impossible air of composure. They opposed the Legion's vastness by charging them head-on, tearing them apart with unbridled ferocity and meticulous coordination.

The madness.

A small shadow rose up, clinging to one of the Reginleif's long legs. The Reginleif raised its legs to shake it off—then gouged it with one of its pile drivers, skewering it through the head.

It was a self-propelled anti-tank mine. Eugene understood this but still shivered in terror at the sight. Was the Processor truly able to discern in that brief moment that this wasn't a friendly troop asking for help? Or maybe he didn't care to begin with whether it was a friendly and acted out of self-defense?

The Reginleif shook its leg, as if trying to get rid of a stubborn piece of trash, and the humanoid figure that had vividly stuck to the leg was thrown away, only to hit a Löwe. Its fuse triggered, and it blew up, the metal jet of its high-explosive anti-tank warhead eating into the top of the Tank type's armor.

The flickering flames illuminated the Reginleif's white armor, making the Personal Mark on it visible for a moment. A headless skeleton carrying a shovel—the ominous mark of the Reaper, the most abominable and maddest of the Processors.

The Personal Mark of the greatest among *them*. As all his consort units had been downed in their first campaign, he alone had defeated the entire enemy force.

His name was—

Eugene's eyes widened in realization when the company captain sitting behind him in the gunner's seat spat out bitterly.

The name of those born of the Republic's malice, tempered by cruelty and polished by ruthlessness. The name of those weapons of slaughter given human form, who were no different from the Legion.

"The Eighty-Six...the monsters of the Republic...!"

Fundamentally, armored weapons—be they treadmill types or walking types—break down significantly less if they are not operated outside of combat situations. Shin took a seat in the cabin of the

Advanced Technology Research Bureau's 1,028th Trial Unit's combat squadron's special heavy-transport vehicle, which carried his Reginleif, Undertaker.

He wore a flight suit in the Federacy military's steel-blue color, with a badge shaped after the national emblem of the two-headed eagle and the rank insignia of second lieutenant. His light-blue scarf was, strictly speaking, in violation of military regulations, but everyone looked the other way so long as he didn't wear it in formal occasions.

He was reaching under his scarf to remove the RAID Device from his neck when he received a Sensory Resonance call from the maintenance crew in the rear storage box compartment.

" **"Second Lieutenant Nouzen." "**

"You've still got the wireless switched on, Corporal."

He could hear him click his tongue from both the Resonance and the speakers.

" **"Right, shit. I can't get used to how different this Para-RAID thing is from the radio. Why'd they have to stick our unit with testing this thing when we've already got this crazy machine to work on...? Anyway. About your ammo refills, you're fine with half cast explosives and half armor-piercers, right?" "**

The majority of the Nordlicht squadron was made up of soldiers from the old combat territories of Vargus and wasn't officially in the army's register. When the Federacy was still the Empire, the Vargus were warrior-class slaves stationed in combat territories on the cusp of the Empire's borders as defense in case of emergency. Generations of life on the battlefield had made them rough and hardened, and the current regime employed them as mercenaries, making their discipline rather lax. They did, at the very least, refer to officers respectfully.

"Yeah, that's fine."

" **"Also, we're out of spare blades. There are fewer and fewer Juggernauts, and you're the only one using that crazy weapon, Second Lieutenant. The next time you sortie, do me a favor and refrain from swinging those knives of yours around like some crazy serial killer, okay?" "**

Calling this machine a Juggernaut—the same name as the Republic drone it was based on—instead of its official name, the XM2 Reginleif, was yet another characteristic of the Nordlicht squadron. Last month, shortly after they'd deployed for their trial sorties, half the squadron—including its captain—died in combat, leaving Shin as the most senior officer remaining and therefore its new captain. He would call the Reginleif a Juggernaut, and everyone else seemed to have gotten used to it because of him.

They all seemed to agree it was a far more fitting name than that of a Valkyrie. Compared to a bringer of salvation, the name of a grotesque, rampaging god was much better suited to an unruly, metallic beast that ruthlessly devoured its test operators during its development and half of its squadron later.

It was because of the Juggernaut's extreme tendency to pick its riders that the Nordlicht squadron, which was, as far as military terminology was concerned, on the verge of being considered decimated, hadn't received any new man power, not to mention had been reorganized since its formation.

"It'll be fine. The Legion should be retreating soon."

" "Huh? Oh, right... That, uh, thing of yours. I don't really get how it works, Second Lieutenant, but it's definitely convenient." "

Closing out with something that was either a word of admiration or him speaking to himself, the corporal shut off the Para-RAID with a twinge of fear in his voice. Shin removed the RAID Device, a metal ring that had a similar, but far more polished and advanced, function to a throat microphone.

And just as he thought it wasn't much different from a collar, a voice that used a tone that went beyond antiquated and straight into the territory of exaggeration spoke to him from the driver's seat. It was the sort of voice that Shin, who knew only the battlefield, thought belonged a century or two in the past.

"A job well done, Shinei."

"...Frederica. You sneaked in again."

A small girl of roughly ten years old leaned back from the seat, facing him. She had slender limbs, a petite frame, and a delicate, doll-like face that looked at him from beneath her military cap. Her gemstone eyes were a Pyrope's red, and her long Onyx-black hair trailed down to her knees, clashing with her steel-blue uniform.

This cheeky girl he'd known for six months now—since before he'd enlisted in the trial unit—puffed up her chest proudly.

"Your attempts to exclude me by mingling with the maintenance crew were in vain, I'm afraid. As they were rather frantic in their final checks, there were ample opportunities for me to sneak in."

"...Corporal. We're gonna need to have a little talk when we get back to base."

"Second Lieutenant...?! No, hear me out here! We really were swamped with work this time..."

Leaving the corporal with that remark as he shut down the wireless line, Shin sighed and looked into Frederica's eyes, red, much like his own.

"I keep telling you, you don't have to follow us on sorties. Do your duties properly, *Mascot*."

"You're very brave or else very foolish to speak to me that way while you act under my command. Furthermore, you've no right to speak of properly performing one's duties. One who presumes to be a commanding officer, no matter how small the company, does not simply leave his consort units behind and charge onto the battlefield. This tendency to leap into the fray unassisted is a bad habit of yours. Bernholdt was complaining about you, I'll have you know."

This sergeant, the most senior member of the squadron and a young man in the prime of his life, shrugged. That silent shrug went to show that while he was displeased that his advice was ignored, he had no complaints from a strategic point of view. Bernholdt had acknowledged that Shin's judgment was sound, so Shin didn't pry any further into the matter.

"It's their fault for not keeping up with me. If I just stood around and waited for them to catch up, it'd defeat the whole point of mounting a mobile defense."

The Processors who'd been left behind all remained silent and smiled wryly at his words. Frederica, on the other hand, simply frowned.

"Mobile defense, you say. Indeed, it is fitting for someone like you. However, I cannot abide by it. Such tactics operate under the assumption that one's line of defense has been breached."

One would have to set infantry units as the front line and hold back the armored units, with their superior mobility and firepower, in the back lines. This defensive strategy enabled them to exterminate the enemy every time they broke through the front lines. As the Legion's fierce attacks over the past month locked both sides in stalemate, they adopted this defensive strategy in an attempt to minimize losses.

"While this may buy us time for the moment, the glaring difference in our armies' reproductive capabilities makes it clear this strategy will eventually fail. And when it does, what do you think will become of you out there on the front lines?"

From Shin's perspective, all of this was said far too late to matter. That didn't concern him in the slightest, so he merely sat in his seat. Did it matter to the troops in the front what happened once this country fell? Did it matter to *them*?

Frederica leaned forward to meet Shin's eyes, displeasure plain on her face.

"Are you listening, Shinei? Your penchant for reckless endangerment is also rather troubling. Have you no concern for your own well-being? Remember that you are no longer a soldier of the Republic's Eighty-Sixth Sector, but of the Federac— Hiyaaa?!"

She let out a high-pitched shriek. Shin had pulled Frederica's military cap all the way down below her nose to silence her prattling. Ignoring her squeals of panic, he leaned back against the hard backrest of his seat and closed his eyes.

The Legion had raided them tonight in large numbers, and they had received more appeals for reinforcements today than they could count. He had plenty of experience fighting over one or two consecutive nights and intended to savor every nap he could take.

Frederica, meanwhile, was still at the mercy of her hat.

"Uuuh, I can't get it off; it won't come oooooff— Bernholdt, help meeeeee."

"Sure thing. But once I do, please quiet down. Everyone, the second lieutenant included, has been fighting for days. Some haven't gotten a wink of sleep, y'know?"

"I see… My apologies."

Feeling a fleeting gaze turn in his direction, Shin surrendered himself to a brief slumber. Even in his sleep, he could hear the mechanical ghosts' wails and lamentations, never once abating as they prowled the lands to the west.

†

FOB 15 served as the advance base for the 177th Armored Division and as the second defensive line for the Federal Republic of Giad's western front line. It was home base for the 141st Regiment. Which meant that due to the large number of officers and Feldreß this base housed, its cafeteria was incredibly spacious.

Eugene carried his tray in one hand through the large cafeteria, scouring the area in an attempt to find the person he was looking for. Since it was rebuilt every time the front lines shifted, the cafeteria was fairly plain and unadorned. If it were ten years ago, before the revolution, when Giad was an empire rather than a Federacy, there would no doubt be portraits of past despots hung here. But instead, the Federacy's national policy, "Strive to be the justice the world prides itself on," and its crossed flag adorned the walls.

"Mm. If you're looking for the Nordlicht squadron's officers, I believe I saw them over there."

"Thank you."

"Making the effort to understand and accept our newcomers is an admirable gesture, young Second Lieutenant. The Eighty-Six have had it harder than most, after all."

This captain, who appeared to be a former noble of Sapphira blood, flashed Eugene a toothy grin. Eugene responded with a vague smile of his own and bored his way into the jumbled crowd of people that filled the room. The captain's words were true, but Eugene still found Eighty-Six other than Shin—not that he'd ever met another one—to be strange and scary. If he were to call out to them normally, perhaps talk with them and get a feel for their personalities, maybe he'd think they were decent people, but…

The Federacy was a multiracial nation. Its military bases were full of people from all walks of life, but there was a lot of disparity when it came to the soldiers' ages, and young men and women in their late teens stood out in the crowd. Eugene was one such example, a young officer who'd graduated from a special military academy. He was part of a system where after receiving the minimal secondary education, he was appointed as a second lieutenant. He then began his military term and gradually received the higher education that normally would have been mandatory for him to receive prior to enlisting.

This system was installed by the Federacy as a last resort to ensure there would always be officers, even after ten years of grueling war with the Legion. However, it did have the benefit of paving the way for children of middle-class families to become officers, and it was entirely voluntary. No matter how bad the state of the war had become, the Federacy's government had never stooped to forcing the civilians to enlist.

Only the lowest kind of scum would force others to fight their battles for them.

The Federacy was nothing like the Empire or that country to the west.

That said, his roommate and partner in the special officer academy had mentioned that this was also because a makeshift army of conscripts was inefficient in this day and age, and on this type of battlefield, where soldiers were required to have the technical knowledge and skill to operate weaponry.

"…Hey, what're the people from Nordlicht doing here?"

"Our unit called them over for reinforcements yesterday, remember? That Reaper and his headless skeleton… They give me the creeps."

"I heard they downed a crazy number of units in the month they've been here… Both enemies and friendlies."

"I mean, damn, he actually sits inside that thing, doesn't he? The whole Processor thing wasn't some figure of speech, was it?"

"Cut it out, man. If you're gonna say that, how are you any different from those assholes over in the Republic, y'know? Our glorious Federacy doesn't deal in those kinds of atrocities."

"You're not wrong. Glory to the two-headed eagle."

The conversation between those two officers—from the armored infantry forces, judging by their physiques—ironically helped Eugene reach his destination. At the end of a long table in one corner of the room, he found the person he was looking for. He was sitting across from a little girl dressed in full uniform. This young man, clad in a standard military double-breasted blazer, was putting his breakfast in order.

Both had black hair and red eyes, of respectively Onyx and Pyrope origins, and they looked like a pair of siblings only a few years apart. They had the graceful looks that were the mark of the old Empire's nobility, making their facial features quite similar as well. Eugene had heard, however, that the boy didn't have a family anymore.

Maybe the reason their corner was so empty in comparison to the rest of the congested cafeteria was because of their colors. The old nobility prioritized racial homogeneity and abhorred mixed blood, and the middle-class civilians despised the ruling class's descendants. Typically, the Onyxes and Pyropes were of the ruling class, but even if a person had blood from two different noble families, if those families were different colors, that person would be shunned by the nobility.

Another possible reason for their isolation came to mind. Perhaps the rest of their unit simply felt the same way everyone else did about their questionable reputations.

Poking the corner of her tray with a fork, the young girl spoke, her voice like the chirping of a canary.

"…Shinei. Do you enjoy eating mushrooms, perchance?"

"Not particularly. You don't have to force yourself to eat them if you don't want to, you know."

"This is true, however…leaving food on my plate would be most disrespectful to the ones who went to the trouble of preparing it for me, would it not?"

"Then eat the mushrooms."

"Nn…"

Despite his words, the boy shifted the buttered mushrooms from her tray to his, leaving only a small one for her to handle. Curt as he may appear, his nature was that of a kind older brother.

"It's been a while, Shin."

Shin turned and faced him with bloodred eyes, and after one long moment, he blinked.

"Eugene. You were assigned to this base?"

"Since last month."

After asking permission, he took a seat next to the girl. Shin's crimson eyes were trained on him.

"You were a huge help yesterday. That Personal Mark with the skeleton—that was you, right?"

Shin seemed pensive for a long moment.

"Um… Sorry, which unit were you?"

Even though it had happened only yesterday, Shin couldn't remember saving his life.

"Ah-ha-ha, you're pretty active out there, aren't you?"

Looking between the two boys restlessly, Frederica asked:

"An acquaintance of yours?"

"He was my squadmate in the special officer academy."

"We've known each other since before that, though. We both volunteered for the armored division, shared a room during training, formed a team, and even piloted the same unit during Vánagandr training."

Frederica averted her gaze uncomfortably.

"Oh… That sounds…rather unfortunate…for you…"

Eugene leaned forward enthusiastically, his eyes agleam.

"Oh, so you know? This guy's always silent and blunt, and you can never tell what he's thinking."

"Indeed, you speak the truth. He never lifts his eyes from his books when people attempt to converse with him, and if he loses interest in what the other person is saying, he simply nods in lieu of a verbal response. He is not above tuning someone out entirely when it suits him."

"He's usually so distant you'd think he was some cold-blooded creature, but then he goes and does something crazy before you even have time to react. Do you know about Shin's legendary zero-point failure?"

"Oh-ho? Do tell."

"He tried to get a Vánagandr to jump in a mock battle during combat-maneuvers practice. Got himself disqualified immediately for risky piloting."

That was four months ago, at the end of their three-month-long special officer academy basic training. On its own, it was an impressive feat of piloting, but forcing a Vánagandr—which weighed a whopping fifty tons when battle ready—to jump wasn't something the unit was built to handle, not to mention the risk of injury to the pilots inside. Eugene, who'd served as Shin's gunner at the time, had hit his head hard against the headrest, learning firsthand that *seeing stars* was more than just an idiom.

Shin was inherently incompatible with piloting Vánagandrs. It seemed odd to be opposed to the safety of solid composite armor and the power of the 120 mm turret because they were "too heavy," but this incident was what had led Shin to transfer to the 1,028th Trial Unit... Which had left Eugene feeling rather lonely at the time.

But even as his good name was being slandered right in front of him, Shin seemed entirely detached from the conversation and merely sipped on his coffee. No fun whatsoever. Exchanging miffed expressions, Frederica and Eugene both burst out in laughter a moment later.

"Second Lieutenant Eugene Rantz, of the 18th Company. Nice to meet you."

"Frederica Rosenfort. A pleasure to make your acquaintance... Now, then."

Finishing off her own cup of coffee, loaded with cream and sugar (though Shin had snatched the sugar bowl away after she'd scooped four spoonfuls into it), Frederica rose from her seat.

"I didn't intend to be the third wheel to a pair of old friends in the middle of their reunion. I'll be taking my leave."

Holding up her tray, which was intended for adults and still far too big for her petite frame, she nimbly wove through the sea of people and trotted away with brisk steps. Watching her go, Eugene had to address the elephant in the room. After all, such a young girl seemed quite out of place in a military base.

"…So that's your squadron's *Mascot*?"

"Yeah."

It was a tradition dating back to the Empire's rule, which some squadrons upheld to this day, installed as a precaution to keep conscripted soldiers from deserting. They would introduce a young girl—around an age appropriate to play the soldiers' little sister or daughter—into the squadron, giving her shelter and food, all the while trying to have them form a makeshift family. The hope was that the soldiers would be inspired to continue fighting, even to the death, all to protect their beloved "daughter."

"We're like a group of mercenaries, after all. I guess you could say she's a hostage, as the origin story goes."

They weren't *like* a group of mercenaries. That's exactly what they were. For example, Shin was the only registered military personnel in the rescue force that had deployed yesterday. The others were all Vargus, a type of mercenary, and most of the other officers, the squad's commanding officer included, had been killed by the Legion.

"…That's terrible. I can't believe they're still using Mascots in this day and age, and sending her into a unit of Vargus, too…"

"She chose to take this path."

Eugene grimaced at Shin's matter-of-fact statement.

"You say that, but a girl like that doesn't have a reason to fight."

As Shin's red eyes looked back at him suddenly, Eugene felt something nudge at his heart. As if there was suddenly a distance between them— No, that gaze made him realize *the distance had been there all along*. It made him feel as if they weren't in the same place. As if something stood between them, segregating them.

Shaking off that feeling, he said:

"Such a small girl shouldn't have any reason to fight. She shouldn't have anything to defend. No family or country, no justice or way of life. And still... Why should she have to fight? That's messed up, isn't it?"

He closed his eyes for a moment, as if to hide his expression. When Shin opened them again, they still somehow felt serenely closed, and Eugene could no longer sense the wall between them.

"...Yeah, I suppose it is."

Having gone to make a second cup of coffee, Shin also brought one for Eugene, who accepted the paper cup with a thank-you. They called it coffee, but it was a substitute made from barley and chicory. As the Federacy's sphere of influence was surrounded by the Legion and the Eintagsfliege's jamming blocked all communications, any diplomatic relations or trade with other countries was impossible, to say nothing of even being able to confirm one another's existence. As such, coffee beans, which grew in the southern and southeastern parts of the continent, were unobtainable.

"By the way, you had a little sister, right?"

"Ah, yeah. She's a bit younger than Frederica, though."

His hand touched a locket dangling from his neck below his uniform's tie alongside his dog tag.

"...Our parents are gone, see. And I have to earn money if I'm going to send her to a good school."

It had happened six years ago. The war with the Legion had intensified, and they'd had to evacuate their village. The evacuation train to the capital had been too packed for all four of them, and their parents had shoved Eugene and his sister into the compartment, hoping to at least save their children.

That was the last he saw of them.

As they hadn't had the leisure to take any family photos with them, his sister, who'd been a baby at the time, didn't remember her parents' faces.

"She's on summer vacation from elementary school right now, and I'm thinking I might take her out somewhere next time I get leave. A trip might be hard to manage, but the zoo should be easy enough. Oh, I could take her to the department store in Sankt Jeder. Girls like getting new clothes and shoes, right? Ah, now that I think of it, they opened a new café in the capital's department store."

Shin smiled thinly, watching Eugene fire off his options at a mile a minute.

"Being a big brother seems hard."

"Wanna cover my next 'big brother' shift? I totally don't mind."

"Sorry to disappoint, but I've already got a little troublemaker to deal with."

And after he gave Eugene a wry smile, Shin's expression hardened.

"But if that's the case, are you sure you should be a soldier? The war's not going well right now, and I don't see it getting better anytime soon."

If you've got family to look after all on your own…

Eugene's expression changed at those unsaid words.

"Are you saying that based on experience from your *old battlefield*?"

"…Yeah."

Back when they were in the special officer academy, Shin told him about it. Part of the training program was to deploy cadets out into real combat. In practice, they sent them out on patrol in field uniforms and with assault rifles, equipped with old-fashioned gear. It was only a task to get them used to the battlefield and build up their nerve, but as luck would have it, they were raided by the Legion. Eugene made it back only because he was paired with Shin.

That was when he asked. How was Shin able to tell how the Legion were going to move…? How was he so used to the battlefield? At the time, Shin looked pensive for a while before eventually answering. In that same detached, indifferent tone, he told him…

…of his past.

The story of how he survived the death his homeland had sentenced him to.

However, Eugene never did find it in himself to ask about the mark on his neck—a scar so gruesome that it looked as if he had once been decapitated. A scar from an act of cruelty, inflicted on him out of pure malice.

Eugene realized Shin was concerned for him only because he was that familiar with the horrors of the battlefield and the intensity that came when fighting the Legion. That made him happy. Shin never said much, rarely concerned himself with other people, and could be extremely hardheaded, but he wasn't a bad person. Even with that terrible past behind him, he still befriended an Alba… A pureblood like Eugene.

"But… Well, yeah… I guess."

He took a sip of his coffee and grimaced. Bitter. He'd forgotten to put in sugar.

"Just yesterday, ten guys died in our squad. We did manage to expand our territory little by little over these ten years, and even this place was established last spring over land we reclaimed. But people are still dying all the time."

When the Federacy was still the Empire, its territory spanned from the continent's northwest to its north-central region, expanding to the west and east. It was a superpower that boasted the largest landmass and population on the continent—and was a militant nation at that.

Shortly after the Federacy was established, the Legion began a reverse invasion of their lands, and the Vargus protecting the country's lands fulfilled their role loyally. While the Federacy was cut down to less than half of its combat territories, this allowed it to keep the territories focused on production and the capital—which served as the nation's core—unharmed.

It retained most of its national power and was able to gain data on the Legion's performance by examining what few specimens still

remained in the Empire-funded laboratories, on top of combat knowledge it had accumulated over ten years of fighting the Legion.

Backed by these factors, it mobilized against the Legion and was
able to just barely match them, even gradually making headway and
regaining lost territory. The nation's public safety and the expansion of
its territory were gained by vastly consuming the Federacy's national
power and the lives of its soldiers. The Legion, which operated without fragile, treacherous components like pilots, exceeded the Federacy's
weapons in many ways.

On top of that, the Legion, which were created with an unchangeable
life span set into their central processors, were able to overcome this sole
limitation by assimilating the neural networks of dead soldiers—Shin
called these specimens Black Sheep—which enabled them to perpetuate
endless war and slaughter without anything to hold them in check. It was
also confirmed that the Legion went on active Headhunts, where they
sought out living humans to assimilate their neural networks before they
went into a state of degradation. Which meant that it was the Federacy,
not the Legion, that was on a timer.

"From what I saw yesterday, other squads aren't much different. I'm
almost surprised the Legion didn't make it past the second defensive
line."

"The commanding officers were saying that this many casualties are
to be expected when things get bad. The western front is the Federacy's
largest, fiercest front. The 177th Armored Division's sector is one of the
most contested zones on the western front, too."

The Federacy's northern, southern, and eastern borders had their
first to fourth fronts blessed with mountainous terrain with high elevation and a large river. They were natural fortresses, making it easy
to hold a line of defense in those areas. The only front that was hard to
defend was the western one, which was covered in vast plains, making
it difficult to beat back large numbers. The front extended for four hundred kilometers, with the forces stationed there being four times the size
of the forces deployed in each of the other fronts.

"To be expected, huh...? I only have one month of experience on this country's battlefield, but I don't think that number of casualties is something you can just shrug off like that. The Legion's losses just don't match ours. Considering we're still holding the line, we're losing too many troops."

"I agree. It doesn't really feel like we're winning here. The commanders might just be used to this, but the military's upper echelons are all former nobles. To them, the number of commoners that die on the battlefield is just a fluctuating statistic. To them, it's no different than sending livestock to slaughter."

The realization of what he had just said hit him, and he pursed his lips. The person right before his eyes was treated like livestock by the Republic and wouldn't even have been counted as a casualty to begin with.

"...Sorry."

"Hmm? What for?"

Shin made a dubious face, and Eugene simply waved his hand, dismissing the subject. If he didn't get it, that was fine. There was no point in stirring up painful memories.

But.

It was then that Eugene wondered. If that was really what happened to him, why did Shin return to the battlefield?

Shin didn't have a family. They were all stolen away from him by the Republic that should have been his homeland, and he alone was left alive. He wasn't native to the Federacy and didn't have anyone to protect in this country, no ideal to uphold by defending his homeland or comrades. And with the government granting him aid and support, he didn't even need to work here to get food or shelter.

So...why?

"Umm...Shin."

"What?"

"Well... I mean, I could ask you the same thing you asked me earlier."

Should he really ask? Eugene fell into a hesitant silence. Shin's red eyes suddenly shifted from Eugene, his gaze glaring in another direction. He looked far away, beyond the base's thick defensive walls, as if seeing something well beyond it. The atmosphere around him chilled immediately, making Eugene hold his tongue.

"Wh-what's…?"

And just as he was about to ask "What's wrong?" the blaring of a warning siren silenced his words.

This alarm meant that self-propelled, unmanned reconnaissance probes that were deployed in the contested zones had detected the presence of the Legion. The Legion had been developed by the Empire, but its successor, the Federacy, employed only these reconnaissance probes as their sole unmanned machines. Higher education was monopolized by the aristocrats, who made up the core of the dictatorship, and the lower nobility.

The Federacy, however, emphasized the middle classes and couldn't match the Empire's overwhelming technological advancements. The lead researcher who'd effectively invented the Legion's advanced artificial intelligence had passed away before the war even broke out, and the Federacy failed to develop a fully independent AI capable of matching the Legion.

And even if they did, the government and the civilians all agreed that they would not employ such a tactic. Fighting to defend the country and their brethren was both the duty and right of the people, and they wouldn't let machines take that away from them. Many people were also deeply traumatized by the lethal capabilities of rogue autonomous machines—a horrific reality that they were forced to confront every day of their lives.

After a long moment of tense silence, the two stood up as the cafeteria filled with suspense and confusion.

"Those stupid hunks of scrap never let up. It's one day after another. This isn't going to score them any points with the ladies, dammit."

"The Auto Reproduction types are called Weisel, which means *queen bee*. That makes the rest of the Legion worker bees, so technically, they're all female."

"So they've come to court us Federacy soldier men, huh? They're so clingy it makes me wanna cry."

As they reveled in their dark humor, they left the cafeteria only to part at the hallway. Eugene's armored division and the research division Shin tentatively belonged to as part of the trial unit had different chains of command and different hangars.

"I'll see you later."

"Yeah."

It would not be an exaggeration to call the Federacy's western front an obstacle course, with its narrow forested zones and city ruins that could be established as battle zones. These areas would be the focal points in strategies to defeat the Tank-type Löwe, which served as the main force of the Legion, and the Heavy Tank–type Dinosauria, which were sent to break through defensive lines.

But this decision did not always benefit the Federacy. For the Vánagandr, whose massive frame was just as large as the Löwe's, this terrain was very difficult to maneuver in. And if one became cut off from coordination with its consort units, this kind of terrain could prove fatal if it was cornered by a group of Grauwolf types.

They were in a forest filled with the conifer and broad-leaved trees native to the western front. Pursued by Grauwolf types that attempted to cut into his unit from all four directions, Eugene spurred his Vánagandr forward. The silent forest trembled at the force of the fifty-ton unit's steps as its propulsion system moaned in agony.

The Legion washed over the Federacy like a tidal wave, no matter whether it was night or day. Their raids were irregular and intermittent yet relentless. They repeated these attacks, steadily exhausting the Federacy's stamina and morale, and once hostilities commenced, the battles would continue for half a month. The Legion could employ this strategy because, unlike humans, who took roughly a year to reproduce, the Auto Reproduction–type Weisel, which lay deep within Legion territory, could churn out new units with the same speed and fluidity as the jet-black smoke billowing from their exhaust vents.

The sky over the battlefield was blanketed by the silver filament of the Eintagsfliege clouds, which jammed the radar and data link, and the Long-Range Gunner-type Skorpion's bombardment sporadically rained down on the entrenched soldiers. In terms of individual capabilities, the armored infantry was no match for the Grauwolf, and the Vánagandr wasn't quite equal to the Löwe, which meant the Federacy would have to use coordinated strategies to overcome them. But the Legion—ever living up to their ominous name—had the overwhelming numerical advantage, which allowed them to overcome the weakness of their lack of sophisticated tactics.

At times, Eugene had thought, *Are we going to lose?*

We—the Federacy. Or perhaps all of humankind. Were they going to lose to these murder machines who had no reason to war against them? Would they eventually lose the strength to fight, and one day lose—

"Second Lieutenant Rantz! Quit daydreaming! Do you *want* to die?!"

Those words were accompanied by a kick from the gunner's seat, jolting Eugene from his thoughts. The radar screen was covered with the Legion's red blips. The information system just barely remained online, projecting information regarding the combat status of the other units on the holo-screen.

The battle wasn't going well. The armored unit, which was in charge of mobile defense and was to be stationed in the second defensive line's rear, was nearly standing on the front line. Shin's Nordlicht squadron was deployed nearby. It attacked the flanks of the charging Löwe, repelling their advance in a melee engagement that didn't distinguish between friend or foe. As that took place, the armored units, who had been at the head of the offensive until now, took this chance to reorganize themselves and commence a counterattack in coordination with the Nordlicht squadron.

Shin's squad would always appear on the battlefields that needed it the most, which also happened to be the most dangerous ones. As the wreckage of the destroyed Legion scattered over the battlefield, friendly troops also died like flies, their dead bodies piling up until they created a mountain of corpses.

The Nordlicht squadron would always plunge into the most terrible hells any sane person would recoil from, and they would do so without fear. Eugene was aware there were people on the front who mockingly called them demons in human form and said they drank the blood of the fallen for sustenance. The headless skeletons, who bore the name of the Valkyrie, the decider of life and death on the battlefield, charged into combat once again, lured by the scent of their slain comrades.

Suddenly, white noise rushed through all their optical screens and multipurpose holo-windows. The value on the screen indicating the Eintagsfliege's density changed. The electronic jamming had intensified.

And just before the noise completely drowned out all their comms—the Nordlicht squadron's blips began retreating at top speed, and a voice yelling something into the open line only barely registered in Eugene's consciousness.

Something rained down from above—and burst. Shock waves ripped through the air. In this age, when even sluggish, recoilless rifles fired bullets that traveled faster than the speed of sound, the roar of explosions always came last.

A shower of steel washed over them.

Sensory Resonance, which traveled via the collective unconscious, wasn't affected by the electronic jamming that silenced all manner of wireless communications.

"Are you unharmed, Shinei?"

"Yeah."

"Thank goodness..."

But as she said that, Frederica's voice trembled.

"...However...I am afraid I have bad news."

*   *   *

Looking down at the smoking steel-colored wreckage that had been ripped apart by the hail of self-forging fragments, Shin opened his mouth to speak.

"Frederica—close your 'eyes.'"

When Eugene opened his eyes, he was met with greenery hanging over him. Green oak and beech leaves gently wavered overhead. Spruce and pine trees cast a dark-green shadow over him. The emerald of the foliage mingled with the Eintagsfliege's thin clouds, catching trace rays of sunlight and rendering the mist slightly transparent. Green painted over the very fog, the hazy iridescent shades of a northern forest's summer.

Feeling the grass, moist with dew, against his cheeks told him he was lying down on the ground. He could make out the massive gray silhouette of a mechanical carcass that resembled a giant beast—his shredded Vánagandr—crouching a short distance from him.

A slender shadow knelt next to him. Eugene strained his eyes to make out who it was.

"Shin."

Shin's bloodred gaze looked down on Eugene. His cold, serene gaze never wavered, not even now. If the Grim Reaper existed, his eyes would surely look like that.

"The commander...?"

"He's dead."

"And...me...?"

He vaguely knew he was beyond saving. If there was any chance of helping him, Shin wouldn't simply be looking down at him like this.

"You don't want to know."

"Tell me."

Shin gave a long, resolute sigh.

"Everything below your stomach is gone."

He could tell he wasn't just cut up. He could imagine how bad it was from the blood on Shin's steel-blue flight suit. He looked as if he'd trudged through a river of blood.

Really… He wasn't a bad guy. As inappropriate as it was, Eugene found himself smiling. Even though he knew it was hopeless, Shin had still pulled him out of the wreckage. And judging from how he didn't feel even a tinge of pain, Shin must have administered him morphine, too.

He'd wasted precious painkillers on a dying soldier.

But Eugene was still grateful he'd pulled him out of the Vánagandr. He didn't want to die stuck in that sealed cockpit, choking on the stench of his own blood and entrails.

"Shin… I've got to ask you for one last favor."

"What is it?"

"I want you to take my locket. I'm wearing it just under my gear…"

Shin's eyes wavered slightly when Eugene realized he no longer had the hands to complete the task. Removing his gloves, perhaps not wanting to dirty them, Shin reached out to take the locket. After a moment of hesitation, he reached into the flight suit's collar, his fingers clasping the cold metal object. It slowly heated up, taking in Shin's body heat.

As he rose to his feet, towering above Eugene like a great black crow, Shin retrieved a pistol from the holster on his right thigh. He pulled back the slide and put a bullet into the chamber. It was a 99 mm automatic pistol, larger than the ones the Federacy provided its pilots. It was a weapon that was completely ineffective against the Legion's armor.

Eugene's hands would have probably shaken too much to complete the task if he'd been put in Shin's position, and yet, neither the muzzle nor the gaze directed at him wavered in the slightest. But he knew by now that it wasn't out of coldheartedness.

So the least he could do to repay him was to muster the last of his strength and force a smile.

"Sorry… Thanks."

A single gunshot echoed across the battlefield.

*   *   *

Frederica had said he was still alive, but she'd never told Shin to save him. That had made the situation perfectly clear.

"Fido…"

He called out to his faithful Scavenger, only to remember he'd left it behind in the Legion's territories, as he'd been unable to take it back, and closed his mouth. Once this battle ended, Eugene's corpse would be recovered, sent back to his family, and given a proper, dignified burial. Probably before his soul—or something similar to it, if such a thing existed—returned to the darkness at the edge of the world.

But his name, his final expression, his smiles, and the stories of the family he often spoke of were etched into Shin's heart. Along with those of the untold hundreds that he had accompanied to the end until now.

That was always the only thing he could ever really do.

As he broke off one of Eugene's two dog tags for the sake of his death report, Shin heard a heavy machine's loud footsteps approaching him. It wasn't the Legion. Their highly efficient propulsion and buffering systems made it so even the Tank types didn't make noise when walking, and besides, he would know if the Legion were approaching him.

Before long, he saw a damaged Vánagandr bearing the 18th Company's insignia of a porcupine approach him through the emerald fog.

Noticing the totaled Vánagandr and the corpse of his comrade, along with the young soldier who served another unit, the operator of the last remaining Vánagandr from the 18th Company brought his machine to a halt.

He was standing in an abandoned corner of a dangerous battlefield where there was no telling when the Legion might attack. He didn't even have an assault rifle for self-defense on him, but oddly enough and despite the recklessness of it all, the boy's silent posture didn't seem to give off any sign of crisis.

Lying hidden near the broken Vánagandr was the boy's own unit, a white, four-legged Feldreß, waiting on standby. The operator swallowed nervously. A Reginleif. The headless skeleton that appeared only in battle-fields of countless casualties.

The boy didn't have his headset on, so they couldn't talk via wire-less. The unit's commander cautiously opened the canopy of the back, gunner seat. The young soldier cocked an eyebrow, looking up at him. The operator gave a small moan.

"Nouzen…!"

They'd been in the same class at the special officer academy. He was one of the more gifted recruits in a program that consisted mostly of chil-dren who'd been sent off by their families to reduce the number of mouths they had to feed. His grades in combat drills were head and shoulders above everyone else, but he was pawned off to some trial unit for repeated disciplinary violations and breaching of orders.

Rumor was that he'd been sent to some disciplinary unit filled with mercenaries from the combat territories to test a suicide weapon.

Shin had also been the roommate and teammate of Eugene Rantz, another one of their classmates… And the operator swallowed nervously yet again when he realized the half corpse lying nearby was that very same Eugene.

"Good timing. Could you report his death for me?"

Catching the dog tag Shin casually tossed his way, the gunner asked: "Did you euthanize him?"

He figured as much from the pistol in Shin's hand and the puddle of blood that spread over the undergrowth. It was usually the job of mili-tary physicians to decide how to treat the injured, but war wounds being what they were, situations often arose when it was obvious some injuries were beyond medical treatment. In cases where the injured would have likely succumbed to their wounds on the trip back, putting them out of their misery on the spot was seen as an act of mercy.

Shin nodded. The gunner, his face a mix of conflicted emotions, parted his lips to thank him when the other soldier, the operator, shouted.

"Why didn't you save him?!"

Shin didn't answer. He simply looked back at him with cold, calm bloodred eyes.

"You knew it was Eugene, right? He said he met with you this morning before we sortied. So you knew it was him, right?! Why didn't you come to save him?! You didn't mind butting into other units' fights and wrecking everything in sight, did you?!"

Within all units that were charged with mobile defense, the Nordlicht squadron boasted the highest number of kills, which was only natural, since they charged into contested zones other units would shy away from.

They were that strong, and yet.

They'd been rescued and given refuge by the Federacy. They had no reason to keep fighting, and yet!

"You probably prioritized killing those hunks of scrap over saving him, didn't you?! You war-obsessed Eighty-Six!"

Eighty-Six.

That was the name his homeland, the Republic of San Magnolia, gave them when it defined them as pigs in human form, before the Federacy rescued them. The name of those five young soldiers who made it to the edge of the Federacy's territory after they'd been sentenced to death on the battlefield.

Shin was silent.

The gunner grabbed the operator's shoulder, stopping him from saying any more.

"Knock it off, Second Lieutenant Marcel. Are you trying to be as horrible as those scumbags in the Republic?"

Marcel fell silent at the gunner's admonition. He knew that the atrocities the Republic had committed against its citizens, the Eighty-Six, had been widely reported on national television six months ago, when Shin and his group had been found.

He didn't want to be anything like the Republic. But...

The gunner lowered his head, his hand still gripping Marcel's shoulder.

"I apologize for Second Lieutenant Marcel's impolite words. And allow me to also extend my thanks for the mercy you've given Second Lieutenant Rantz, as well. Thank you. And I'm sorry."

"...It's fine."

Looking at Shin, who merely shook his head, the gunner continued.

"Perhaps you volunteered with the Federacy's military to return the favor for our saving you. But you don't have to do that."

"..."

"We, the Federacy, will never surrender to the Legion. We will rise to the task on the battlefield, and we will uphold our sense of justice. We fight of our own will to defend our families, our homeland, our comrades, and the ideals of this country. We won't force you poor children to fight for us... It isn't too late. Retire from the army and live a life of happiness this time."

Shin's only response was a cold glare.

But the next moment, he looked away. Answering a superior officer—albeit of another unit—rudely by turning his back, he said only one thing, with ice in his voice.

"The Legion are coming. Regroup with the rest of the force, immediately."

Sitting in the cockpit of his Juggernaut, Undertaker, Shin scanned over the multipurpose windows, trying to discern the state of the battle. By now, he'd already pushed Eugene's death to the back of his mind. Five years on the battlefield had made this machinelike behavior second nature to him.

Suddenly remembering he had it turned off, Shin switched on the Para-RAID, activating his Sensory Resonance. He wouldn't have minded if it was the other soldiers, who had made war their livelihood since the time the Federacy was still the Empire, but at the very least, he wanted to spare Frederica from having to witness the death of someone she knew. He'd made that clear and hoped she wouldn't look anyway.

The moment Shin turned the Para-RAID back on, Frederica began speaking. She'd probably been waiting for him to reconnect.

"Shinei."

"What's our status?"

The integrated information system's data link was still severed. He could sense the Legion's positions to an extent but was blind when it came to where any *surviving* friendly units were. He would have to infer that from the enemy's movements but didn't know the Federacy's terrain well enough to do so, and there were far too many consort units deployed for him to make guesses. Asking someone overlooking the battlefield would be faster.

"Unfavorable. Our main force has fallen back to the secondary line to regroup. The bombardment from earlier has crippled us greatly."

"Do you have detailed information on the damages?"

"I'm still able to *see* several squadron leaders, however... We're doubling as the command vehicle, but the data links are off-line for the most part..."

The Eintagsfliege had deployed in several layers, effectively killing their data links. The antiaircraft guns they deployed to disperse them had their advance blocked by Skorpion fire.

This is rough, Shin thought, his expression unwavering.

The Federacy's war potential was significantly larger than the Republic's. Every weapon system they deployed to the battlefield was well-made. They also had artillery and data link support, but...even so, the Legion were much stronger. The only reason the Republic had survived for nine years was because the majority of the Legion's forces were sent to fight the Federacy. Or perhaps the Legion simply treated the Republic as nothing more than a test site.

"—We've received an update from Division HQ. Once we begin our counter-attack, the Nordlicht squadron is to raid the Legion from the flank. Regroup at coordinates 27–39 and remain on standby until further notice... They had to run a messenger to deliver this message. What a dreary state of affairs..."

"Roger that."

He rotated Undertaker's bearing and set out. Before long, Bernholdt regrouped with him, and they were joined by their two remaining platoons shortly after. The squadron's surviving units converged around them from all over the battlefield, the blue blips marking them on the radar screen slowly moving their way. And just as a blip with a familiar Personal Name approached him, there was a voice he hadn't heard for a while on the battlefield.

"They don't gather the whole squad like this every day. What, have the Vánagandrs all been done in already?"

Wehrwolf.

Regarding the squadron code and machine number that appeared on the screen, Shin answered the voice that connected to him through the Resonance.

"Raiden... How did the reinforcements go on your side?"

"Sad to say, but the standard armored unit is pretty much wiped out... The guys up there are expecting us to mount a counterattack, but I wouldn't anticipate much help out of the main force, the way things are."

"...Not that we were counting on them to help anyway."

"I mean, here we are again, with the counteroffensive failing and our army isolated. They tell us to raid them, but it's more like they want us to cut through the front lines and act as bait."

"I guess when they tell you to fight your way out of a bad situation, it's all the same no matter where you are."

His fellow Eighty-Six spoke up one after another, appearing from their stations throughout the battlefield. The familiar names appeared on the radar screen as it crackled from the powerful electronic jamming. Looking at those names, Shin sighed. Even after reaching this country, war had remained the same as ever.

When they'd ventured beyond the battlefield that had claimed countless souls, they hadn't known that what awaited them was more of the same war. They hadn't expected to step back into the same hell.

Back then, when they'd set out on the death march known as the Special Reconnaissance mission—

CHAPTER 2
PANZER LIED

The Special Reconnaissance mission was surprisingly peaceful, and they continued to make progress well beyond its expected duration. Maybe decimating that platoon on their first day of the mission had paid off. If they were to make it out of the contested zones, they would make it into the territories the Legion recognized as their own. Their patrols would become more lax.

Shin's ability to know the Legion's location and discern the direction they were moving in allowed him to pick routes where he and his group wouldn't run into the patrols, or they would remain hidden until they passed by. They made their way east, avoiding battle whenever possible. They camped out as the season turned to autumn, eating tasteless synthetic food, and continued marching through enemy territory, not knowing when death might claim them.

That journey was their first ever taste of freedom.

The Legion's territories had once been inhabited by people and were dotted with villages and cities—however abandoned. When they had the chance, they would search through these ruins and hunt livestock that had gone feral. When circumstances allowed, they would light fires they could huddle around during their nightly camps, appreciating the gradual change in scenery of the towns and the natural view around them, which no other humans could see any longer.

It happened when autumn's presence grew thicker, and the ruins lost all marks of the Republic, becoming more associated with the Empire.

They had reached their final destination.

"Fido."

"You're proof. Proof that we reached this place. May you carry out your duty until you crumble into dust."

Shin, who had been genuflecting until now, rose to his feet, looking at Fido's side, which had been hit by bombardment, silencing it forever. Did that final order reach the broken Scavenger? Could its meager intelligence, designed to do nothing else but collect trash and scrap, understand the meaning behind Shin's words?

Shin turned around and returned to Raiden's side.

"You all right with this, man?"

Pausing for a moment, Shin realized what Raiden meant; the aluminum grave markers Shin had etched the names of their dead comrades into. He'd only just decided to leave all 576 names—Rei's name included—here in the wreckage of the Juggernauts, alongside Fido.

"Yeah. Now that it's come to this, we're not going to last much longer."

Everyone, excluding Fido, had survived their latest battle, but they had lost all the Juggernauts except for Undertaker. Now, when the only weapons they had left were the small firearms they carried for self-defense, they didn't have any means of fighting the massive Legion. When the time came for them to fight their next battle, it'd be all over for them.

But knowing this, Shin gave a faint smile and knocked on Fido's charred container with the back of his hand.

"But I want to repay him for everything... Since we can't take him along any farther."

The loyal scavenger who would bring him the bits of armor to etch the names of the dead on was gone now, after all. Raiden managed a thin smile. To think that after all this time, they were staring their demise in the face.

"Looks like our fun little hike is coming to an end, eh?"

Taking a deep breath, Raiden wiped away his smile and looked to the west—the direction they had come from. They could see a single patch of steel-colored sky hanging over a battlefield. Yellow petals fluttered through the air, riding the wind. Ahead of them was a set of rails, divided into eight: the remnants of transit used by the people who once inhabited this place.

"But damn, there's so fucking many of them..."

"...Yeah."

They had somehow slipped through the depths of the Legion's territories, and just as Shin once guessed from the mechanical moans he could hear, a countless number of Legion inhabited them. No matter which direction they looked, the Legion filled the plains like a silver mosaic, leaving no gap. A swarm of Löwe and Dinosauria stood on standby. Swarms of Recovery Transport types, the Tausendfüßler, went back and forth in pairs from the back lines of the battlefield like a surging river.

The Eintagsfliege perched on the trees of a withering forest, covering them like frost. If one was to wander inside, they would find the place's mineral resources had been mined out, leveling the mountain into a crater and leaving the dug-up ground rust red, a nightmarish rendition of hell on earth. That was probably the work of the Auto Reproduction types, the Weisel, and the Power Plant types, the Admiral. Their frames were so massive they couldn't be properly perceived, but Shin and the others could just barely make them out, crawling through the fog.

They had seen the Legion's massive army moving through the territories, as they had to sometimes spend days hiding beneath the cold rain. And they knew that there was no resisting such a large army of mechanical ghosts.

The Republic would lose this war. Perhaps all of humankind would.

—Would the day come when *she*, too, reached this place?

Anju returned, having finished connecting the container to Undertaker with a winch and wire. They had stored what supplies they had left into the last container and had Undertaker tow it.

"Job's done, you two, so let's go. If we stick around too long, other Legion might come inspect the noise from the last battle and track us down here."

Shifting his gaze, Shin caught sight of Kurena and Theo hopping down from the container and Undertaker, respectively. They had been helping Anju. From here on out, they would advance while taking turns piloting Undertaker. They had agreed earlier that if they got attacked, whoever was piloting Undertaker at the time would fight the Legion while the others ran for cover so as to not get in the pilot's way.

After stretching once, Theo put his hands behind his head and frowned.

"But man, to think the one Juggernaut that survived was Shin's… It's set to work on Shin's parameters, so the controls are hella sensitive. Piloting it scares the shit out of me. Most of its limiters are broken, too."

That was the reason Undertaker was capable of performing maneuvers that would usually be impossible for a Juggernaut. Of course, Shin's piloting skills, which were extraordinary even among the Name Bearers, were also a major factor in enabling those stunts.

"I'll go first, then." Kurena raised her hand in an oddly excited fashion. "I was downed first earlier, so I'm not tired."

While it was still functional, Undertaker was beginning to show signs of not having been properly serviced in a long time. And despite the danger of piloting a unit she wasn't accustomed to, Kurena had the machine rise to its feet. Sitting on top of the towed container, Shin suddenly realized a Legion was following them.

It wasn't attacking them, for some reason. It may have been a scout assigned to track them, but it wasn't calling any other Legion. A lone Legion, following them from behind, as if it was trying to ambush them. When they stopped, so did it, and if they were to turn around, it would likely do the same.

The Juggernaut's armaments were short-range, and it could attack only things within its range of sight. They had no means of attacking a Legion hiding beyond the horizon, and it didn't seem to engage them, either, so Shin kept it quiet from Raiden and the others. Judging from its voice, it was a Shepherd, but it was oddly muffled, and Shin couldn't tell what it was saying. But it was somehow familiar.

Where did he know that voice from—?

†

Not being able to die when death came to claim you was a peculiar fate.

So Rei thought, dragging his barely functioning body as if by the very strings of his failing nerves, made of liquid micromachines.

In order to preserve data, the Legion's mission recorder was set to transfer the battle data from a downed unit's files to a nearby consort unit. In the case of a Shepherd, it would transfer everything—the central processor data included—to a spare unit prepared and designated ahead of time.

Black Sheep, which also used humans as components, could exist in multiples, but there existed only one of each Shepherd. That was because Shepherds had their own individual personalities and could not stand having another individual bear the same existence. However, the Legion couldn't afford to lose a Shepherd's high performance as a Processor and prepared a transfer system that moved their consciousness into a spare unit.

That said, Rei found the mechanism to be pretty much pointless.

Safely transferring data files the moment a unit was about to be destroyed left them damaged. A perfect transfer was nearly impossible. The majority of the data didn't survive the transfer, and even if it did, the spare unit barely functioned. Torn to pieces by the cast explosive's metal jet, Rei's data files were left in a tattered state of disrepair by the time the transfer had completed.

He wouldn't last long.

And perhaps because he knew this, he tracked Shin's progress through

the territories. Keeping a safe distance so he wouldn't be discovered...
He resolved to see his brother's final destination. He dragged the bat-
tered, creaking fuselage of the spare Dinosauria he inhabited.

The thought suddenly occurred to him that he probably was Shourei
Nouzen's soul, after all. His data files were disintegrating with every
passing moment, but for some reason, the memories of that final battle
remained whole and clear.

He remembered how his instincts as a war machine blended his
desire to protect with the desire to kill. He remembered the illusory silver figure of the girl who blocked his way, as if to shield his target from
death. He remembered the voice that would still call him Brother, even
after the countless lives he'd taken. He remembered it all.

Shin and his friends advanced into the territories, evading battle
and slipping through the gaps in the Legion's patrols.

That's good, Rei thought. *Don't think of battle. Just focus on staying
alive for even a second longer. The Federacy is up ahead—humankind's
greatest hope, which faced the Legion valiantly even as it stood surrounded
and isolated.*

If he could just reach the Federacy, Shin would surely be given refuge. Unlike the Republic, the Federacy's troops were all upright and
decent. Soldiers of different colors fought back-to-back and wouldn't
leave their comrades abandoned on the battlefield, even if they were
reduced to corpses. They would never treat five children who'd escaped
death's maw cruelly.

And by the time that happened, his sense of self would be all but gone.
And that was for the best. Even if he still had a grasp on his sanity now, he
would go mad again at some point. The desire to kill would paint afresh
over all his desires and wishes...and he would once more call for Shin.

And if Rei were to call out, Shin would surely come to seek him
out again. He would not abandon his stupid older brother, who selfishly
killed and selfishly died. Rei's kind little brother, who wandered through
the hellish battlefield for five long years, would come to put him out of
his misery.

I'm sorry. This time, I'll go to the other side properly. So please, just let me see this through to the end.

The Dinosauria marched on, each of its steps driven by nothing but prayer.

†

"—Anju. Switch with me."

Anju, who was in the middle of piloting Undertaker, blinked at the words Shin sent her way via the Para-RAID.

It had been two days since they'd bid their final farewell to Fido and the fallen comrades Shin had entrusted it with. They were in the midst of a forest, the autumn sun streaming down the foliage, illuminating the deciduous leaves and maple seeds.

"Isn't it too early? Wasn't the noon shift supposed to last until we stop for dinner?"

"I'm bored."

That point-blank, blunt answer made a smile play over Anju's lips. True enough, Shin wasn't one for idle chatter, and with nothing to do but look at the scenery, he was probably bored stiff.

"We've got too much free time on our hands. You should have at least taken some books to read."

Smiling wryly, Anju reached for the cockpit's unlocking lever.

†

Rei's gradually fading thought processes filled with relief as he watched Shin and his friends approach the Federacy. If they kept going, they would be within the Federacy military's patrol lines soon. The Legion focused all their forces on battling the Federacy near the patrol lines. A single, small mobile weapon should be able to avoid detection so long as it used the terrain to hide itself.

Rei wasn't sure whether he would expire before seeing them arrive at civilization but... Well, they should be fine. He could pass on peacefully— Nnn!

A string of information from nearby friendly units had arrived via his barely functioning data link. And as he perceived the contents of that message, anxiety flared through Rei's nervous network.

Oh no...!

†

As they approached an animal trail leading down a slope steep enough to be called a cliff, Undertaker suddenly stopped. Raiden, who was lying down on a blanket he had carried back from his unit, sat up.

"What's wrong, Shin?"

Shin responded coolly. It was his usual quiet tone, but there was a ring of silent resolve in it:

"—Whoever's piloting at the time fights. That's what we decided."

It took Raiden only a moment to understand.

"...You ass! You *knew* they were coming!"

He'd noticed a group of Legion ahead of them that they couldn't avoid no matter what route they took... Probably since the moment he'd asked Anju to change places with him! Anju jumped off the container, her hair standing on end in anger.

"That's not fair, Shin! You can't do this!"

Anju tried to approach him, but Shin purged the tractor wire connecting the container to Undertaker. Anju recoiled as the wire flicked away violently, and Undertaker took that chance to use the difference in elevation to bound up the slope. It was steep enough to be a cliff and wasn't the kind of distance a human being could scale easily. There was no detour in sight, which was probably why Shin chose this route.

The Juggernaut's cracked optical sensor swerved their way. It had lost both its grappling arms, and its armor was scorched and burned. Its propulsion system was faltering, and the machine in general looked to be covered in wounds.

"You guys keep going. They shouldn't find you if you head into the

forest... The Legion's forces die out a bit farther from here. If there's people there, ask them to shelter you."

They'd already heard him say something like this once, in the battlefield of the Eighty-Sixth Sector. And it was natural they wouldn't find them. So long as they detected an enemy unit—that is to say, Undertaker—within their territory, the Legion would turn their focus on it. Perhaps Shin had planned even that.

"Screw that! That just means you'll be playing decoy for us!"

"Weren't we supposed to go together?! You can't just decide to go on your own at the last minute. That's—"

Shutting off the Sensory Resonance to cut out Theo's shouting and Kurena's tearful voice, Undertaker disappeared into the trees.

Raiden punched the container with all his might.

"God *dammit*...!"

Whoever was piloting when they encountered an enemy would be the one to fight. They'd decided this would be a fair way to determine who would fight the last battle, a way that would leave the others satisfied no matter who ended up with the responsibility. But they'd been too naive. If Shin, who could sense the Legion from afar, recognized an enemy they couldn't avoid, it would be tantamount to him implicitly condemning whoever was piloting at the time to death. And to avoid that, he would simply have to make sure he was the one sitting at the helm.

"That idiot...!"

Raiden stood up, grabbing the assault rifle next to him.

†

As they were fulfilling their standard patrol schedule, a Legion patrol company suffered an assault from a unit of unknown affiliation. After updating their Friend/Foe ID, the patrol company opened hostilities while transmitting its combat status over the data link.

This armored weapon fought while ignoring all conventional strategies. Downing a Löwe by bombing it in a surprise attack, it dived into the heart of the formation. There was no match for this enemy unit in their native data, but the wide area network's database had a match for the model.

The Republic of San Magnolia's primary weapon system. Identifier: Juggernaut. Its threat level was low, and both its armor and firepower were weak by armored-weapon standards, but it was comparable to armored infantry. And when fighting on plains with few obstacles, this weak land weapon would have no means of penetrating the Löwe's solid armor.

At least, it should not have been able to, but this Juggernaut exhibited combat prowess that exceeded all assumptions. Bringing the battle into melee range, it used the Löwe armor to shield itself from the other Legion's fire and used its weak firepower to shrink the distance up to point-blank range.

The Juggernaut was intended for melee combat. Its specs were no different from other specimens, so there was only one difference that could influence its combat capabilities so much: the performance of its central processor.

Four defending Löwe were destroyed. Forty-five percent of the company's forces were decimated. And yet, the mechanical demons didn't feel a shred of impatience.

Redesignating target's threat level. Target determined to be equal to the Federacy's main weapon system. Type: Feldreß. Identifier: Vánagandr. Chances of suppressing the target with current forces deemed unfavorable. Requesting reinforcements and support from main force and nearby units.

Special addendum: *Capture of target advised.*

Transmitting the report and request for orders to the wide area network within milliseconds, the Legion set out once again.

†

…The enemy's movements changed.

Shin realized that after he'd defeated the fourth Löwe, the Legion shifted their deployment patterns. Both his eyes and his consciousness darted around nervously. When encircling an enemy, it was common knowledge to deploy the units of one's force in such a way that they did not get caught in each other's cross fire. And that should have applied just the same for the Legion, even if they did not hesitate to gun the Republic's forces down along with their consort units...

But these Legion blocked his path, even if it meant that their allies got caught within their line of fire. They were stalling him. And as if to affirm that realization, Shin's ability informed him that nearby Legion were beginning to move in his direction. The distance to the closest enemy force—probably this patrol company's main force—was four thousand meters from here. Taking a Löwe's cruising speed into consideration, they would likely have Shin within their range in less than a minute.

If they linked up with the main force, even Shin would be in trouble. Dodging the charging Grauwolf slashes, Shin opened fire and used that momentary gap in their formation to break through the encirclement. His armor shrieked as heavy machine-gun fire grazed it, and an indicator lit up in his machine-status system. His rear left leg had passed the permissible damage limit.

So that was what the Legion were after...

Shin's eyes narrowed bitterly when he realized it. They were after his "head." They were going to make him a Black Sheep or a Shepherd. The Legion would assimilate the neural networks of dead soldiers and—

Shin sensed something. Even Shin, who was the most senior among the Processors, didn't expect to find *it* here. And that was to be expected; he'd encountered it only once, and it was impossible to distinguish it from others within a crowd. Shin had said so himself once before. This unit was meant for complete suppression of a wide area, and it wouldn't fire only to down a single target.

But he could feel its gaze fixed on him now.

Far away from here, from beyond the range of even the Skorpion fire, he could feel a deep malice, as if he was being glared at by a cold black eye, frozen in rage.

`"I'll kill them."`

*   *   *

Perhaps it was because their words were so similar, but for a second, Shin wondered whether he'd failed to kill his brother. The tone was that similar. He flashed back to the night when he was nearly killed.

Blind terror froze his hands gripping the control sticks.

I'll kill them.

Fragmented images flowed into Shin's subconscious. Memories that weren't his own. It was like the Sensory Resonance or perhaps like the ability he had that allowed him to peer into others' minds when they were connected.

A cloudy sky. Ruins. Shattered flagstones. And suspended vividly in the distance, with only gray as its backdrop, a bloodstained mantle, small enough for a child, dangling like a hanged sinner.

I'll kill them.

Be they men or women or children or the elderly, aristocrats and commoners alike.

Everyone, every single one. Without exception. I'll kill them all…!

He knew this voice. He knew it from the Republic, from the Eighty-Sixth Sector, from when he fought in the first ward as part of the Spearhead squadron. Four of his comrades died in that battle. It was the one that blew them to pieces, from far beyond the range of the radar—

"…!"

Was it his warrior's instincts or the fact that he had experienced this attack once before that made Undertaker leap aside? The impact came at the same time that the radar blared out its alert. Traveling at an ultrahigh speed with an initial velocity of four thousand meters per second, a barrage of shells with a weight of several tons each rained on the battlefield, wrapped in a massive amount of kinetic energy. The shower of steel fell mercilessly into the Legion's patrol company.

The explosion was so loud that Shin was convinced he had gone deaf. A white light flashed over the battlefield, inhibiting his line of sight. The powerful shock waves launched the shell's fragments in all directions, eating into the Legion's armor, ripping through them, and blowing them away. The bombardment scattered large chunks of soil and sedimentary rock about, which crashed back down on the battlefield like a meteor shower, carving craters into the ground.

The autumn field was reduced to scorched earth in the blink of an eye.

Blown away by the deafening explosion and maelstrom of force, Undertaker just barely avoided the shell's effective radius. But he was far from unharmed. His main motor was critically damaged by stray fragments that flew into the cockpit. His gyro and cooling-system indicators faded from the gauges, and all his holo-windows had shut down.

He was lucky to still have his propulsion and weapons systems online. There were still enemies around. Performing damage control almost unconsciously with one hand, he ignored the busted main screen and tried to trace the enemy's position—

At that moment, his rear leg's joints flew off, no longer able to bear the weight of the dying Juggernaut.

"—!"

He just barely managed to maintain balance with his remaining legs. But that was the most he could do. The Juggernaut's main battery, located at the back of the fuselage, was extremely heavy, throwing off its center of gravity so much that it leaned backward. If it lost any of its rear legs, the Juggernaut was entirely incapable of walking.

The old familiar cussing of an aging maintenance worker echoed in Shin's ears.

"I keep tellin' ya the suspension unit's weak, so why d'ya keep pushin' it like that?! . . . That crazy fightin' style of yours is gonna get ya killed one day!"

And here it comes.

Bursting through the curtain of smoke and sediment, a Löwe charged toward them even with half its legs blown off by the explosion. Looking up at the machine's front leg, which was swinging overhead and preparing to descend on him, Shin cracked a smile.

*   *   *

Undertaker was flung back by the blow, pieces of its fuselage scattering into the air.

Finally locating a section of the rock face with decent footholds, Raiden and the others scaled the cliff and followed the sound of gunfire out of the forest, only to be greeted by that sight. It was the first time Raiden ever saw their Reaper lose.

His instincts were screaming at him in self-preservation—there was no way a human could beat a Löwe on their own. And his sense of reason tried to hold him in check—if they were to come out now, Shin would have died in vain.

Fuck that.

Standing stock-still for no more than a second, Raiden broke into a run, as if propelled forward. Spurred on by the sound of his comrades' footsteps beside him, he charged through the forest.

Stirred by loud assault rifle fire, Shin just barely raised his heavy eyelids. All his optical screens and gauges were completely dead, and the interior of the toppled Juggernaut was dark. It hurt to breathe. A burning sensation filled his lungs, and his ragged breath smelled of blood. It didn't seem as if he was bleeding anywhere, but he felt extremely cold.

He realized, belatedly, as if it were someone else's problem, that he had sustained internal injuries. If he was indeed still alive, he should probably do something—at least pull out his pistol and end it all—but he couldn't lift a finger.

He could hear the sound of gunshots and the shouting of the comrades he'd abandoned from the other side of the thin, flimsy armor. A part of him thought they were idiots for doing this, but he also thought he couldn't mock them. Now, by doing the exact thing they were doing, he had landed in this situation, after all.

It was foolish and meaningless—much like this war—and yet, it was a good death, the kind he would have wished for. An inappropriately wry smile played over his lips again. He had managed to slay his brother and had come much farther than he would have expected. There was nothing left unsaid.

...And yet, perhaps because it was a moment like this, he realized he didn't want to die.

Would he be assimilated by the Legion?

And if he did become a Legion, whose name would he call?

Not a single face came to mind. That was his sole regret.

The screams and gunshots suddenly cut off. Shin's ability informed him a Legion was reaching out to rip off the canopy.

Tungsten bullets penetrating through thick armor and the screeching of metal.

Those were the last things Shin heard before his consciousness sank into nothing.

†

Five enemy targets neutralized.

The only remaining Löwe sent this report to the Sector's network. It also sent a recommendation to have the prototype—which had offered supporting fire—recalibrated. Despite the recommendation to capture the target, it had fired with the intent to destroy and annihilated a company of friendlies all to terminate one enemy Feldreß. Its processing units' capacity for sound judgment was lacking, it seemed.

After sending its message, the Löwe turned its optical sensor to the downed Juggernaut. It, like the other four Processors, hadn't been destroyed to the extent of its vital signs being terminated. The enemy Processor was brittle, and while extraction and scanning could damage the tissues, once it died, they began degrading. As such, acquiring it alive was the optimal choice.

The hostile element boarding this Juggernaut was an extraordinary Processor unit, capable of turning the tide of battle despite the machine's low performance levels. If it were to be provided to a friendly unit, it would contribute to the war effort immensely.

Combat-oriented Legion like the Löwe had no means of transporting materials, so it sent a transmission through the wide area network, requesting a nearby Tausendfüßler to carry the specimen over to a nearby Weisel.

And then it happened—the Löwe detected an approaching friendly unit and shifted to IFF (Identify Friend/Foe) mode. It was a Heavy Tank type that wasn't currently assigned to any force. The Löwe that had detected it fired, and—

A large blast enveloped the battlefield.

The Löwe's thick composite-steel armor, capable of even withstanding a shell from a fellow Tank type's main armament at point-blank, was mercilessly penetrated by 155 mm armor-piercing rounds.

The Dinosauria had just fired at the Löwe. The automatic machine knew neither fear nor surprise, but it took it a moment to assess the situation. What had just happened should not have been possible for the Legion. Had the Dinosauria mistaken it for an enemy? Impossible. They'd returned each other's IFF signatures.

It had attacked the Löwe while aware that they were both of the same army. In other words, it was an enemy.

It used old-type tungsten bullets. If it had been a high-explosive anti-tank warhead or a depleted uranium shell, the internal explosion would have downed it in one blow. The Löwe refreshed its IFF information, designating this Dinosauria as a hostile unit. It sent the report of this engagement through the data link and prepared to face the—

Another attack.

A consecutive barrage of high-caliber shells ripped the Dinosauria's barely functional central processor to shreds. It fired so as not to generate any secondary explosions—so as not to allow any harm to befall the nearby Juggernaut. The crumbling Löwe had no way of knowing that was why the Dinosauria fired armor-piercing rounds and not anti-tank warheads.

The last thing the Löwe's cracked optical sensor perceived was the strange sight of the Dinosauria extending a hand made out of liquid micromachines—

†

Shin was dreaming.

In that dream, Shin was a small child, and when he came to, someone was carrying him in their arms. Just the two of them, without another soul around, walked through shapeless darkness. It was the same darkness he could always hear beyond the mechanical ghosts' wails, the boundless void at the depths of all perception, at the depths of the soul.

Shin looked up, only to see his big brother. He looked a bit *older* than he remembered, about twenty years old... This was probably how he'd looked on the day of his death.

"Brother...?"

Rei smiled. It was his nostalgic, gentle smile.

"You're awake."

Rei stopped and knelt down, placing Shin on the ground. His young body's head was too big, and it made it hard to stand up straight. He was able to steady himself after a few attempts, and he looked up at his brother again.

"This is as far as I go. But after we part ways, don't just keep running off on your own. You've got some great traveling companions, after all."

Still kneeling down and looking deep into young Shin's eyes, Rei continued.

"I can't believe how much you've grown."

Looking down in surprise, Shin found he was once again in his sixteen-year-old body. He tried to say his brother's name, but his voice wouldn't come out. There was no speaking, no communicating with the ghosts. Returning Shin's silent gaze, Rei's face took on an expression of deep sorrow. His hands ran over the scar on Shin's neck. Just like that night and just like that battlefield, his brother's big hands ran across his neck.

"I'm sorry… It must have hurt so much. And my refusing to die and calling you all this time brought you here."

Shin wanted to say he was wrong, to at least shake his head in denial. But he couldn't move his body whatsoever. And saying it didn't hurt would be a lie. It hurt to have his brother direct such pure hate toward him. It hurt to hear his brother's voice calling him out night after night, reminding him that he was at fault for everything that went wrong in their lives—because of his *sin*. It hurt to relive his own "death" countless times in his dreams. It hurt to be plagued by the inescapable screams, always, always reminding him that he would never be forgiven.

But still, it was because of them he'd made it this far. He could withstand the days he spent fighting the Legion in a fruitless, endless struggle on the battlefield where he was sentenced to die and the nights of bitter loneliness as his comrades perished one after another only because he had the goal of killing his brother to keep him going.

If he hadn't had that, he would have fallen on the battlefield a long time ago. It was because he was always there, waiting for him beyond death, that Shin still lived. There was so much he wanted to say—

But the words wouldn't come out.

"You don't have to obsess over me anymore. You can just forget about me."

No…

"Ah… Okay, I lied. I would like you to think about me from time to time. Just as long as you live your own life freely and find happiness. Then, while you're living your long, happy life, maybe sometimes…"

Brother.

Rei laughed.

"I won't wait for you this time… I'm not *that* patient, you know. You still have a long life ahead of you… Just take care of yourself. And please be happy."

Rei's hands let go of him. He turned around, walking to the other end of the darkness, the edge of the abyss his mother, father, and countless comrades had fallen into. And once he got there, they would never meet again.

The spell binding Shin's body suddenly faded.

"Brother."

But his outstretched hand never reached Rei. Perhaps he'd never even heard his voice. An invisible something segregating the living from the dead blocked Shin's path, stopping him from going after his brother.

"Brother!"

Rei turned around with a smile as the darkness enveloped him. This was the same as how he couldn't grab his brother's hand at the end of that battle. He knew he would never make it, but he still reached out.

"Brother."

The sound of his own voice roused Shin from his slumber.

He found himself looking up at a dull artificial ceiling. Shin blinked his hazy red eyes. An unfamiliar white ceiling. Four equally white walls surrounded him, and some device with a monitor was beside him, emitting loud electronic beeps at regular intervals. A heavy scent of disinfectant hung over the air.

He was lying on a sanitized bed in a small room, with the monitor's cord and an IV connected to his body. Shin, who had been in a concentration camp ever since he was small and had hardly received any medical treatment in his life, had no way of associating all these things with the fact that he was in a hospital room.

A burning sensation welled up in the back of his nose, prompting him to hide his eyes with his left hand, for fear of someone seeing his expression. The emotion that washed over him was a mix of deep relief and an equal measure of loss. The fragments of those memories flared up, filling his field of vision.

He remembered. Finally. That, in truth, he never wanted to lose him.

Along with the IV, there was some kind of sensor attached to his left hand, and it triggered an alarm the moment he moved it. But it was an alarm with no sense of pressure to it, meant to inform that a monitored patient had woken up.

The wall opposite the bed lost its white color, becoming transparent, and from the other side, a middle-aged man in a suit peeked into the room. He wore silver-rimmed glasses, and his black hair was streaked with gray. This Jet man had a certain scholarly air.

A nurse appeared behind him, watching him through a transparent "wall" that seemed to serve as the door connecting his room to the equally inorganic-seeming corridor. He could see similar doors opposite him and on both sides of the corridor, so Shin assumed other small rooms were lined up here.

"...I see you've finally come to your senses."

The man spoke in a gentle voice that reminded Shin of someone he had forgotten. Shin wanted to ask something, anything to make sense of the situation, but his voice wouldn't come out. Assailed by sudden pain, Shin moaned, and the nurse knit her eyebrows.

"Your Excellency. He's only just come to and still has a fever due to the side effects of the surgery. Please don't—"

"I am well aware. I merely wish to exchange a few words with him."

Soothing the nurse with a calm smile, the man placed his hand against the door. *That's a soldier's hand*, Shin thought through the haze. It was the hard, thick palm of a man who was used to handling a gun. The silver ring on his fourth finger oddly left an impression in Shin's memory.

"Good day, my boy... To start, would you mind telling me your name?"

Normally, answering that question required very little thought, but it took Shin a long time to fish it out of his memory. His thoughts were all jumbled up. He didn't understand the situation he was in well enough to realize this was all the effect of anesthesia.

A fragment of a memory flickered in his mind—once before, someone else had asked him that question. He recited the answer he'd given then, the long, silver-haired illusion of someone he'd never seen before brushing against the back of his eyelids.

"Shinei…Nouzen."

The man nodded once.

"I am Ernst Zimmerman, the Federal Republic of Giad's temporary president."

†

That day, the Federacy's government-sanctioned news program informed the public that while patrolling the western front, the Federacy's military had found and rescued five young soldiers presumed to belong to another country.

The Federacy's frontline troops had destroyed a Dinosauria thought to be deployed on a Headhunt, only to discover it carried the five of them. Based on the field uniform they were wearing and the OS of their unknown Feldreß, it was presumed they were soldiers associated with the Republic of San Magnolia, their western neighbor.

The Federacy's civilians were filled with excitement. At long last, they had hard proof that they were not the only surviving country. They were not alone. And at the same time, they were concerned, worrying for the safety of their neighboring country. They were no doubt quite desperate if they had to send *children* to the battlefield.

But when the children were questioned and the contents of their interviews were released to the public, revealing the reason they'd been present on the battlefield in the first place, that concern turned to anger. However, worrying for the children's well-being remained very central in the public's eyes.

Those children were persecuted by their homeland but still fought on, escaped, and made their way here. If nothing else, they should be allowed to live peaceful, happy lives in the Federacy.

†

"—That sums up how you came under the protection of our army, but do you remember the events leading up to you being where we found you?"

Having been asked that question and having to come up with an answer made Shin, whose mind had been hazy, slowly regain lucidity. Recalling what had happened before he lost consciousness, Shin suddenly looked around, his gaze turning left and right.

Realizing what had riled Shin up, Ernst laughed.

"Ah, sorry, sorry. You were asleep, so there was no way of communicating this to you, but… Yes, that's right. You would be worried, wouldn't you…? Give me one second."

He turned around and said something to the nurse. The walls to the left and right lost their color, becoming transparent and revealing similarly artificial-looking rooms adjacent to one another. And in the four rooms neighboring his own were his friends. Raiden, who sat in the next room, looked at him with relief in his eyes before grimacing.

"You slept for three whole days, you moron."

His voice came from the speakers in the ceiling. Shin wondered about the Para-RAID, and then he noticed. It wouldn't activate. The back of his neck, which was where the quasi-nerve crystal was implanted, stung with a faint pain. The ear cuff, which the Processors were incapable of removing on their own, was gone, too.

"…Why?"

It was a question without a subject or a predicate, but everyone seemed to understand what he meant. Raiden shrugged.

"Beats me. We've been cooped up in these rooms since we woke up, too. They said a Dinosauria captured us, but…I don't remember seeing one of those."

Shin recalled his dream. His brother had been possessing a Dinosauria, but…Shin couldn't feel his presence anymore. And for some reason, he knew Rei was truly gone. But he wasn't inclined to say it, so he simply shook his head, conjuring up a powerful sense of vertigo. Theo frowned anxiously, noticing how Shin closed his eyes, fighting back the pain.

"Don't push yourself if you still feel bad. You were in intensive care until yesterday. They said you need total peace and quiet for a while… Poor Kurena was crying her eyes out until yesterday."

"Was not!"

Everyone ignored Kurena's fervent cry of objection, though it was easy to see that her eyes were still red. Anju, who sat in the farthest room, smiled at him gently like a pale flower in full bloom. Shin turned his gaze away from her, realizing that was what she looked like when she was terribly angry.

"Shin? I realize it's too soon right now, but once you get better, expect a good slap, okay?"

"Yeah, we're all gonna have to line up and smack you one. Like, hell, if you ever pull a stunt like that again, I'll beat the shit out of you, I swear."

Hearing Theo say that without hesitation, Shin frowned.

"…It's not like I *intended* to die."

"Don't piss me off. Even if you didn't *intend* to die, you knew there was an extremely high chance you'd get yourself killed if you went out there. And you did it anyway."

Acting as bait for the Legion in that state should have been nothing short of suicide, especially taking the immense damage to the Juggernaut and the shortage of ammunition into account.

"We had all considered doing that at one point or another. And that's exactly why we can't forgive what you did. We get it. You can tell where they are and react accordingly, but that doesn't mean you can just make group decisions on your own. It's not fair… Never, ever do that again."

"We were so worried about you."

And as she said that, Kurena's eyes filled with tears again. Entrusting his head to the pillow, Shin closed his eyes.

"—I'm sorry."

Ernst, who had watched over their conversation in silence, spoke with a smile.

"It may feel like we're holding you captive, but we have
to take these measures to prevent a possible biohazard. Rest
assured, we won't treat you poorly. After all, you are our first
guests from abroad since the country's founding.

"—Welcome to the Federal Republic of Giad!"

Ernst spread his hands out in a jesting manner, only to be met by
cold, unreceptive gazes. He shrugged, as if not paying it much heed.

"Well, that's the gist of it. It seems none of us have
a full grasp on exactly what happened out there, but if you
remember anything, do tell us."

Raising an eyebrow, Theo shot his hand up, and he seemed poised
to say something, but Ernst simply smiled.

"You can take your time to remember, for now. I'm sure
talking for too long is hard on you right now… And this scary
lady here looks just about ready to bite my head off."

The nurse, standing in the back and emitting a silent intimidating
aura, glared at him.

Like the president had said, staying awake for long was too hard on
Shin's injured body, and he fell asleep soon after Ernst left. Seeing Shin
fall asleep without saying too much to them made Kurena burst into
tears again, which prompted Anju to start comforting her. Theo began
teasing her as well—his own brand of comforting. When she'd woken
up three days ago and found Shin wasn't with them, she'd wept bitterly
and remained prone to crying ever since.

It's only natural, thought Raiden as he sat on his bed in his prison
cell of a room.

If one were to ignore the fact that they were locked in, they weren't
treated too badly. They got three meals a day—decent ones, at that—and
the rooms and beds were hygienic to an almost superfluous degree. Their
questioning was also extremely reasonable. They treated their injuries,
even Shin's, who was in a condition severe enough to require emergency
surgery. If this had been the Republic, he would have been left to die.

But that didn't mean these people could be trusted.

They were treated as pigs in human form by their homeland, so they knew better than to simply trust in their fellow man. They weren't innocent enough to believe this place would offer them unconditional aid and shelter just because they'd made their way here. They would remain here, like sardines stuffed in a can, and once they gave up all their useful information…would they be disposed of?

Either way, they weren't going anywhere for the foreseeable future. Shin still needed the medical assistance they offered. What was more, this would be a crappy place for their story to end. So thought Raiden, heaving a sigh as he looked up at the ceiling of his windowless room. He missed the sky.

The Federacy's public consensus was one of pity toward the children, but those who were in charge of the nation's well-being couldn't decide things based solely on sympathy and compassion.

Entering the Hospital Module from its adjacent Shelter Module, Ernst walked into an examination room that served as an impromptu conference room.

"What are the results of the analysis?"

The Shelter Module, which was isolated for biohazard-prevention measures, was built so it could also double as a prison and had surveillance cameras and monitors in every room. A holo-screen presented integrated data and its analysis results, and one of the intelligence department's analysts answered Ernst's question.

"In terms of them being spies from the Republic of San Magnolia or some other country, I think it's safe to say they're clean."

The children were on the alert, but it wasn't a product of training. For example, the analysts were capable of surmising the power relationship within the group by paying attention to the frequency of their idle chatter and how often they mentioned one another's names or how much attention they paid to one another. And it seemed the children weren't aware that they were being analyzed in that way.

And if they'd been trained to be able to deceive electronic measures, there would be no point in sending such proficient spies into the Legion's territories. The Republic and the Federacy hadn't even been aware of each other's survival to begin with, because of the Eintagsfliege's electronic jamming.

"They're a bit too alert, but from what we can hear, I'd say it's natural given the treatment they're experiencing. One of the boys, Raiden—he seems to be their subleader—is very much on edge, but that's understandable, what with the state their leader is in. We are effectively holding them captive, after all."

It wasn't particularly their intent to do so, and since the children were receptive to their questions, there wasn't much of a need to, either. But them being cooperative wasn't out of trust, but rather because they didn't want to be questioned more violently should they refuse. The Republic, however, didn't seem to be a place that any of them would be willing to lay down their lives to protect.

"One more thing. Is there any chance of them being a new type of Legion or of being infected with some kind of biological weapon?"

"We'll only have a definitive answer once we get all the test results back, but from what we have so far, in conjunction with the preliminary medical exams from when we brought them in, we haven't detected any abnormalities. But the Legion members don't use biological weapons or devices that mimic humanity, right?"

The Legion didn't produce or utilize any biological weapons— namely, those of the viral or bacterial variety—or weapons that imitated organic life. It seemed they were strictly prohibited from doing so. It stood to reason that the Legion types were made by the Empire to be weapons of domination rather than extermination.

For this reason, having them employ biological weapons that harmed both friend and foe, or humanoid weapons that were hard to distinguish from average civilians, was prohibited. This was always why the self-propelled mines were—despite being humanoid—rather badly disguised.

As a side note, the Legion's definition of biological weapons was one that went too far, as even an unregistered person with a knife could qualify as one. An anecdote was that this was the reason why the old Empire's army never deployed humans onto the same battlefield as the Legion.

But that said, the Legion's control system, namely their tactical/ strategy algorithms, were heavily encrypted, and when they were defeated in battle, they were set to fry their internal mechanisms, making them undecipherable. Ever since they'd begun assimilating the neural networks of dead soldiers to overcome their life span programming, the Federacy had employed great caution.

"The only things that showed up in the scan were those organic devices, which, according to them, are some kind of telecommunication tool. There are some Pyrope families that have the rare ability of communicating telepathically with their blood relatives. The device artificially simulates that phenomenon."

"That's groundbreaking technology."

"Yes. Between this, their testimonies, and the data on the Legion's territories from their mission recorders, I'd say we've gotten more than enough out of them, even if they do turn out to be spies."

The Eintagsfliege's jamming was constant across all the Federacy's front lines, rendering wireless communication impossible.

"As for the machine we recovered—the Juggernaut, I believe it's called—its specs aside, the combat logs are priceless. I believe the boy that serves as their leader was the one piloting it? Once he recovers, I would love to exchange a few words with him."

"Oh dear. The technical-research institute already has heavy investment in our newcomers. I plan to have all of them serve as my test Operators, and I'm afraid we have no intention of relinquishing them to you. These soldiers experienced high-maneuverability skirmishes, and their combat data should go toward the development of my new prototype. Their talents would be wasted on those hunks of metal you call Vánagandrs."

"What did you say, spider woman?"

"I beg your pardon, drone beetle?"

"If you wish to speak with them, you may do so later, with their approval, of course. But this talk of making them Operators will simply not stand. We will be better than the Republic."

With Ernst's plain admonition of a common enemy, the bickering officers fell silent.

"Effort should be rewarded, and they deserve peace for all the fighting they've been forced to do. If their homeland will not give them that peace, then the Federacy will do what is just, for these are the ideals humankind should embody."

One military officer in the west wing of the room opened his mouth to speak.

"...Disposing of them would be safer for the Federacy."

"Lieutenant General, I believe that discussion is already behind us. And you've consented to shelter them as well, if I recall."

"I did. But just as you see justice as the only absolute, the military's first priority is the nation's well-being, Your Excellency. And I fully intend to carry out my duties and oversee these young soldiers' fixed period of isolation and examination."

"Very good. But you did have the soldiers who rescued them placed in isolation as well, yes?"

There was always the chance they were asymptomatic carriers. And besides...

Ernst cracked a tired smile.

"In the first place...our hands are so full with the Legion that we haven't even had a chance to decide on what to do about their immigration procedures."

Presently, those concerned were working to hastily write up appropriate laws and draw up the necessary documents.

†

"This being the case, you five will be citizens of the Federacy starting today."

"...You show your face for the first time in a month, and the first thing you say is 'This being the case'?"

Isolated in a room of acrylic plates, Raiden spoke sarcastically. Not out of the caution the group had initially exhibited toward the Federacy but out of simple displeasure.

And who can blame them? Ernst thought, his smile not changing even in the slightest. These children had so much energy and no chance to make use of it. They'd been confined to these rooms for a month, gradually becoming more and more fed up with repeated examinations and questionings. They would naturally grow bored and frustrated. On the contrary, seeing a glimpse of the youthful nature that suited their age was encouraging.

"For the time being, I will serve as your legal guardian. Take your time to rest and see what this country has to offer, and consider your futures after that."

Their futures.

They'd been informed of their release beforehand and been asked whether they had any specific desires for their future course. Ernst had already read the report containing their responses; they had all requested to be enlisted in the military.

Maybe the person in charge hadn't explained it properly. Maybe they'd misunderstood... Or perhaps war was simply all they knew, and they couldn't consider anything else. The nurses, the doctors, and the counselors all sent similar reports. All five of the kids agreed that being cooped up in their rooms made them feel trapped and anxious. Bored stiff. But more than anything, the situation of the war and the Legion's movements seemed to interest them. As if they felt impatient because they weren't where they were supposed to be.

They had finally escaped the iron grip of the Republic, finally escaped the battlefield... But Ernst realized, sadly, that their personal battles were far from over.

Theo smirked.

"You sure you wanna give us that much freedom? Wouldn't it be safer for you to dispose of us? We're just some kids from an enemy country you picked up in hostile territory."

"Do you want us to kill you?"

Ernst's question, spoken with that same pleasant smile, silenced Theo. Ernst understood. He knew they didn't want to die. But a world at war was the only world they knew, and their experiences in that old world were all they had as reference when trying to make sense of this new one. They couldn't be blamed for that.

Shin calmly parted his lips to speak. Ernst was relieved to see his wounds had all healed over the course of the month.

"What do you stand to gain from saving us?"

"If we were the kind of society that needed to think of gain or loss when faced with the choice of saving children or leaving them to die, we would lose something much more precious. Helping one another is a mind-set that's fundamental to maintaining a community... And besides..."

Ernst smiled thinly. It was a cold, cruel smile, terrible enough to even render these children, who had seen hell on earth, speechless.

"...If we have to kill children because they're unfamiliar to us... Because of a one in a million chance they might be a threat... If that's what humankind has to do to survive, then we deserve to be wiped out."

The quarantine rooms' doors slid open, and the children were instructed to change out of their hospital gowns and come out. Naturally, they didn't have regular clothes of their own, so they were given Federacy military uniforms.

Even now, the children remained wary of the Federacy and its honeyed words. Were they going to be taken somewhere else, like a laboratory or a prison? If that was the case, they preferred to run and be shot in the back rather than simply hand themselves over to the chopping block.

Ernst realized this and tried to hide the fact that he knew they were looking for a chance to escape. But at the same time, he ordered the guards to remain alert. They had no intention of shooting the kids should they run, but having them get hurt while they were subdued would be problematic.

They didn't seem to suspect anything until they got on the transport plane, and it approached an urban area. The plane landed in a military base on the outskirts of the capital, and from there, they boarded a civilian vehicle that would take them to the city. It was then that their doubts turned into confusion.

The vehicle left the base's gate and drove along the main street of the Federacy's capital, Sankt Jeder.

"...Ah."

Kurena's eyes were fixed to the window as a slight gasp escaped her lips. Anju and Theo voiced their amazement as well. Shin and Raiden didn't let their impressions show, but they too found it difficult to look anywhere but the windows as they sat still, holding their breath.

They saw people. Many, many people coming and going. People the same color as them and sometimes different colors, too. A young girl walking down the street, holding her parents' hands. An old couple seated at a café's terrace. A group of students laughing on their journey home from school. A young couple asking a clerk questions at a florist's storefront.

Their wide eyes filled with nostalgia, pain, and seclusion. For the first time in nine lonely years, they had seen the wondrously mundane visage of a peaceful city.

"You did well to make it this far, O pitiful exiles."

Their car had stopped in front of a small manor in the corner of a quiet residential area. This was Ernst's private residence, though he usually stayed at the president's official dwelling.

That aside, as soon as they stepped into the entrance hall, they were met with that sudden greeting. Ernst cradled his head with his hand in exasperation as the children froze in confusion. Those extremely confident words that bordered on ridicule were spoken by the high-pitched, shrill voice of a young girl.

The roughly ten-year-old black-haired, red-eyed girl stood on a small platform she had retrieved from parts unknown. She struck a commanding pose, crossing her hands with an air of self-importance, her chin held high.

"The great Giad welcomes the helpless with compassion and mercy.

We do not expect those of such low station to repay this kindness, so you may accept our sympathy and rejoice."

She then pointed directly at Shin. Was her sight keen enough to discern the group's power balance this quickly? Or perhaps—

"You red-eyed wretch! Why do you turn your back to me?!"

"...I was just wondering if anyone else would be joining us."

Shin's tone was decidedly curt. As would be obvious.

"You just closed the door! Do you take me for a fool?!"

Shin didn't answer, which probably stood for affirmation.

"...I suppose I can expect no better from a Republic plebeian... Even with the blood of the Empire's nobility running through your veins, you are still—"

Her scolding stopped abruptly. The girl's red eyes seemed to be *looking* somewhere else.

"...Your neck... What happened...?"

"..."

Shin's breath caught. The bloodred eyes looking down at the girl suddenly grew much colder, the chill of them and awkwardness of the situation causing the girl to flinch. Ernst sighed and opened his mouth to speak. At present, Shin's scar was hidden behind the collar of his uniform. Although Ernst had seen the scar when Shin had first arrived, he'd never asked about its origins.

"Stop that, Frederica. I've already told you their circumstances... You yourself have wounds you wouldn't want others to pry into, do you not?"

"...My apologies."

The girl bowed her head with surprising meekness. Raiden, who was visibly taken aback, turned to Ernst.

"This your daughter? ...Not to be rude, but you could probably work a little harder to discipline the munchkin."

"Ah, well, she isn't my daughter."

"How dare you assume I am the daughter of some petty paper pusher!"

Apparently taking offense, the girl puffed up her chest. She seemed to have found joy in the situation turning to her favor again.

"I am the esteemed—"

"Frederica Rosenfort. Due to particular circumstances, she has been placed under my care."

Ernst ignored Frederica's glare.

"For the record, I made arrangements for her to pose as my daughter. It saves me the trouble of pointless explanation to outside elements, you see. Oh, and you five are also technically my adopted children now. Feel free to call me Dad if you like."

A long pause ensued.

"...I was only kidding. You don't have to look so disgusted..."

That remark even earned him a fresh glare from Shin.

"Well, to get us back on track, you will be living together with her for the time being. Frederica is a touch ignorant of the ways of the world, but I would be happy if you could see her as a younger sister and try to get along."

Frederica's lips curled up into a haughty smile.

"I am the pet you miserable lot have been given to cleanse the pain of war and persecution from your hearts."

Shin squinted his eyes, and Frederica smiled, as if she'd seen through him. And regardless of whether she harbored any ill will toward him, her smile felt like a sneer. Oddly enough, within the layers of the deceptively simple expression, he could also sense a feeling of solidarity.

"Not just I, but all the things this man presents to you are the same. A safe and comfortable estate, a motherly maid, a guardian to serve as your father, an adorable younger sister—

"It is the Federacy's decision to compassionately grant you a replacement for the family, home, and happiness that were stolen away from you... Do cherish me, my lovely older siblings. Let us befriend one another, as fellow victi— Whoa?!"

Frederica screeched as Raiden reached out and ruffled her hair wildly in what might have been his idea of a friendly handshake. Flailing in an attempt to brush off his hands, she ran back and clung to the golden-haired, blue-eyed slender maid standing behind her.

"Teresaaaaa! They're bullying meeeee!"

"Now, now, my lady. I do believe this was entirely your fault."

Mercilessly cutting down Frederica's whining, Teresa directed a smile worthy of an ice queen at Shin and his group.

"I'm sure you're all tired. How about I pour you some coffee?"

Having eaten a slightly early dinner, the kids each went to their appointed rooms and, as expected, fell asleep. *And who could fault them?* Ernst thought as he enjoyed his cup of coffee, alone at the dinner table. A convenient, peaceful city and a home they could relax in were all concepts that had eluded them for far too long. For them, the change in environment likely felt as though they had arrived in a whole new world. Of course they would be exhausted.

Frederica walked into the room, pouting in a dissatisfied manner.

"They've all fallen asleep. I intended to hear their tales of the Republic. What a vapid evening this turned out to be..."

But the deck of cards in her hand suggested that her wanting to speak to them was just an excuse to play.

"Shall I pour you some milk, Your *former* Majesty?"

"Imbecile. I have no recollection of ever abdicating my title. And what is this talk of milk? Do not treat me like a child."

"Kids aren't supposed to drink coffee before they go to sleep."

But with that being said, Teresa—who had finished making preparations for tomorrow morning—walked in, carrying cups of coffee. One for Frederica and one for herself.

"Thank you for dinner, Teresa."

"Think nothing of it, sir. However, kids of that age certainly do have such healthy appetites. It is pleasant to have someone enjoy my meals...for a change."

The glare she shot in his direction implied the contempt she felt for his consistent absences from home due to work. Her complaints of how poor young lady Frederica was forced to eat her dinners alone were still fresh in his mind.

"I apologize... And I will probably trouble you a great deal going forward."

The children knew nothing but persecution and war, malice and death. Getting one accustomed to peace and goodwill was far harder than getting them used to the opposite.

"Perish the thought, sir. Serving you is my duty, after all."

"...Do you see me as a disgusting man for this?"

He gazed at Teresa's features as she looked back at him. The spitting image of the woman he loved more than anything, and yet, his heart was never moved in the slightest when he looked at her.

"Perhaps you think this a foolish act of compensation on my behalf...that I'm using them as substitutes?"

"—I do not, sir."

Contrary to her words, Teresa's voice was cold. Her features, befitting an ice queen, truly were frozen over. Teresa had said that was the only way she could act before him, and he wouldn't have it any other way. He couldn't keep surrounding himself with illusions forever.

"A person can never be substituted. Each and every one holds a unique existence."

Frederica said plainly:

"Even so, there are people willing to settle for illusions. No matter what form they take."

Ernst brought his coffee cup to his mouth.

"And just who were those words directed at, *Empress*?"

"That's..."

Breaking the sentence off, Frederica fell silent. Looking down at her cup of coffee, watching the dark liquid ripple as if it were reflecting her own heart, she pursed her lips.

She'd been surprised when she'd seen his picture and even more shocked when she'd met him face-to-face. His age was different. Half the blood running through his veins was different. The color of his eyes—and most of all the hue and intensity of his expression—were different. So why...?

...Why were they so alike?

They were different people... But in the way he was trying to reject being imprisoned in a cage of peace, their features almost intersected.

"...Kiri..."

86
[EIGHTY-
SIX]

CHAPTER 3

WILD BLUE YONDER

Two hundred kilometers from the Republic's eastern front's first ward was the Federacy's capital, Sankt Jeder, painted white with the freshly fallen winter snow. Shin stopped at the edge of the main street leading to the City Hall Square and looked up at the clock tower, which was hazy from the powdery snow. The snow was shoveled off the city's flagstones in the mornings, and a large fir tree was set in the center of the market square, serving as a decoration for the Holy Birthday.

Shin had never experienced snow like this before. Was it truly the same snow that had fallen on their corpses in some unknown corner of the battlefield, eventually melting away with the coming of spring? It felt odd, seeing it without the sounds of war in his ears, on a peaceful street corner, surrounded by people coming and going.

His breath came out in puffs of white steam, just as it had on that cold day in the ruins of a church plaza. The coat he had received as a gift was warm. Unlike the clothes he'd worn that day.

Shaking his head once, Shin continued his stride through the snowy street.

When he entered the old Imperial Capital Library in City Hall Square, Shin brushed the snow from his shoulders and took off his coat. This place was always heated. It had been a month since he'd begun frequenting the place, and as he walked in, he exchanged greetings with the librarians who he had come to recognize, before going to browse through the bookshelves.

The Imperial Capital Library was built as a five-story-tall atrium surrounded by annexes, and the dome covering it had a beautiful mother-of-pearl inlay, no doubt painstakingly crafted, in the shape of the summer constellations.

Shin, who was currently living a life with no perception of the date, didn't realize it was a weekday afternoon, which was why the place was fairly empty, giving it a peculiar, tranquil atmosphere.

"...Ah."

He suddenly stopped in front of a bookshelf he rarely examined. The children's bookshelf. He paused because one of the books on the lower shelves had a familiar illustration. He took the old picture book, which he couldn't fully remember. What caught his eye was the cover.

A headless, skeletal knight, brandishing a longsword.

That's Brother's—

Flipping through the book, he realized he had no memory of the story, either. He felt as if he somehow knew it, but the synopsis was so common he thought he might have imagined it. A hero of justice who would defeat the wicked and defend the innocent. But as he read through the book's simple composition, he could hear his brother's voice overlapping the words.

He could almost see those two big hands flipping through the pages. His voice would gradually become lower and thicker. And every night, Shin would pester him, trying to get him to read it aloud to him again.

His brother, who was now gone forever.

—I'm sorry.

Rei's true final words came back to life, and Shin could once again see his retreating back, his visage the same as it was when he was still alive.

Hearing the sound of soft footsteps near him, Shin jerked up, looking at the presence that stood next to him. It was a girl, roughly five or six years old. She wore a wool hat and earmuffs, and her silvery eyes were wide open. Realizing her eyes were locked on the picture book, he closed it and presented it to her with one hand. Perhaps being shy, the girl took it after a long moment of hesitation, then turned around and ran off somewhere.

But the next moment, she came back, accompanied by a boy Shin's age. He had silvery hair and a pair of silver eyes hidden behind his glasses. Seeing that, Shin's expression hardened for a moment.

An Alba. A Celena.

He knew this wasn't the eighty-five Sectors, and the person before him wasn't a citizen of the Republic. He knew this, and yet.

"Allow me to apologize. My little sister was being rude."

"...Oh. That's fine—I wasn't reading it."

The boy's expression turned severe at Shin's words.

"No, it's not fine. When someone does something for you or gives you something, you should say thank you. That's something kids should learn from a young age."

The boy pushed his sister's back, encouraging her. She mumbled something in a near inaudible tone and ran off again.

"Hey, wait...! Geez."

The boy then fell silent after receiving a nasty glare from one of the librarians. The sight of a black-haired, green-eyed woman rebuking an Alba boy was one Shin couldn't help but find peculiar. He really was in an entirely different world, after all.

After a sigh, the boy lowered his head in apology.

"Thanks. Sorry. You shouldn't have to see me disciplining her."

He spoke with the same integrity he tried to teach his sister. Shin felt somewhat amused by looking at him. His simple honesty, coupled with his silver hair and eyes, reminded him of his last Handler, even though he'd never seen her face.

"It's all right. Being a big brother seems hard."

"I don't know who she takes after, but she's terribly shy around strangers."

The boy then tilted his head and slumped his shoulders.

"Hmm, this might be rude to ask, but I always see you here at this hour. Don't you go to school?"

On paper, education up to sixth grade in the Federacy was compulsory. Any following education was optional and no longer free. However, this was just on paper, since this system had been established only nine years ago, with the rise of the Federacy. It was upheld in the capital and nearby cities, but other territories still didn't have enough teachers or school facilities constructed.

And of course, Shin, who wasn't a born citizen of the Federacy but an Eighty-Six who grew up in the internment camps and came under the Federacy's protection only two months ago, didn't attend school, either. Though Ernst had told them to consider it once spring came around and they'd had some time to adjust.

"What about you?"

"Huh?"

"If you see me so often here during school hours, that means you frequent the library as much as I do."

The boy gave a bitter, shameful smile.

"Ah, yeah. I don't go to school. Or more like, can't go to school. Former nobles have...all sorts of things to be ashamed of."

After the revolution, the former nobles' statuses were effectively divided into two. The higher nobles, who were involved in enterprises that served as the lifeblood of the nation, like large-scale agriculture and heavy industry, retained their positions as managers even after relinquishing their social status and tax privileges. That was because the Federacy couldn't afford to cripple the industries that were directly connected to the nation's war potential. It was still at war with the Legion and could not afford to lose even an ounce of martial strength.

Likewise, many of the nobles' children, who couldn't inherit their families' headships and served as officers in the Imperial army, retained their positions in the Federacy's military. But on the other hand, all the other nobles were reduced to normal civilians. They never knew manual labor and had trouble even finding employment to begin with, as they were loathed by the middle class. The lower nobles, who didn't even have enough assets to keep themselves fed, were poorer than even the common laborers by now.

"I thought we might be in the same position… Sorry, it really was rude of me to assume."

Shin shook his head as the boy furrowed his brow.

"I don't mind. I'm not a native."

Shin, of course, meant he wasn't a native of the Federacy, but he'd learned from several conversations already that for citizens of Sankt Jeder, there was nuance to that word that meant one was or wasn't a native of the old Imperial Capital region. Explaining that he was an Eighty-Six was bothersome, and if he said he wasn't a native, people would simply take it that he wasn't from this region but from the territories—and not pry any deeper.

Each of the different territories formerly under the control of the Empire had its own cultures, customs, and value systems. At times, even their language was different from the old Imperial Capital region. As Shin implicitly expressed that there wasn't much to worry about, the boy seemed relieved, and at the same time, his eyes sparkled with curiosity.

"Wow, you have Onyx and Pyrope blood, and you're not from the capital? That's unusual… Oh, there I go again. That was rude. Sorry."

The boy cracked an awkward smile as he scratched the back of his head. His silvery eyes laughed behind his glasses.

"I'm Eugene Rantz. It's a pleasure to make your acquaintance."

"—That concludes it, though. In the month since we took them in, they seem to have acclimated to life here fairly well."

Ernst had told the children placed under his protection "Take your time to see what this country has to offer and consider your futures after that" and allowed them to go about the city freely, but he couldn't send them out into the Federacy's unfamiliar streets unattended.

First, he assigned them guides. And once they got used to the city a little, he had officers close to them in age keep an eye on them from afar, with their reports being summed up to him by his secretary. Hearing her report, Ernst spoke from the mountain of electronic documents, not lifting his eyes from the terminal on his desk.

"I see. He spent yesterday reading every book on the military history shelf. The day before that, he was poring over philosophy books. Three days ago, he took a visit to a military cemetery, and today he was reading children's picture books. I still have no clue what criteria he's choosing his interests from, but Shin making a friend is an auspicious event. We should roast red rice tonight!"

"Serving red rice when they have no idea what that means is a bad idea, much less roasting it. For the love of God, don't."

"Will you even go back today, to begin with? Young Raiden showed up earlier with a change of clothes for you, delivered with Teresa's heated complaints. What are you two having these children do?"

His half-Orienta, half-Eisen secretary quipped at him with a disinterested tone, but Ernst ignored her and continued.

"The change of clothes is meaningless. There's a washing machine here, so I wear the same suit every day. Teresa probably just wanted to send her complaints. I'll definitely be heading back today, so you can go home, too. It's the Holy Birthday, after all!"

"My, thank you."

"I should buy some presents on the way back, too. Do you think the Republic also has the habit of giving gifts on the night of the Holy Birthday?"

"I think they do… But who's to say if the children actually remember that?"

"They'll simply have to learn it anew… Now, then. What should I get them…?"

Ernst smiled with genuine excitement, his eyes still not leaving the terminal. It was on short notice, so he probably couldn't prepare anything too special for them, but still.

It had been a month since they'd come to Sankt Jeder, and each of them had begun finding their way of appreciating the peace. Raiden started a part-time job as a mailman on a motorcycle, Anju began taking cooking classes, Theo was going around the city sketching, Kurena took to enjoying window shopping, and Shin was randomly going between libraries and museums. They had all begun to make friends, too.

Ernst was honestly relieved. Surely they would all abandon the idea of enlisting in the military now. They could finally move past the persecution their homeland inflicted on them... They could put the warrior's mentality to rest.

They would no longer be Eighty-Six.

"...I should make preparations for the futures they'll pick come spring."

From outside the window, the sight of the northern capital's winter could be seen as it waited for the light of spring to shine down on it.

The snowfall that had started the previous night stopped around noon, and there wasn't a cloud in sight. A vast blue sky hung over the plaza's white-gray flagstones. Halting his relaxed, leisurely stride, Theo looked up at the great azure expanse above him. The cherry blossom tree at the center of the plaza stood naked and bony, without a single petal, and the clear winter sky could be seen from between its black branches. It was the sight of eternity as it turned into a cracked, shattered form on the verge of collapse.

Theo lowered his gaze, and his eyes settled on a street holo-screen projecting a parliament meeting. On the stage stood Ernst, in his usual mass-produced business suit and glasses. Seeing him make a speech always gave Theo an odd, dissonant feeling. He was a leader of the revolution, and a hero, and had served ten years as the Federacy's temporary president. But to Theo, he was an odd man who would come back occasionally and pester them about his arbitrary curfew, argue with Frederica about what channel they should watch on the television, and make a fuss over silly disputes.

"Just let the girl have her thirty minutes of cartoons" is what Shin and Raiden would always say when he would switch the channel from Frederica's magical-girl show or an episode of some sort of superhero-squad series to a news program or a soccer broadcast.

Theo was only half listening to the speech, but they were discussing something about the Federacy's war situation. An analysis of each front's state and their policy going forward. Ernst may not have been the one doing the analysis himself, but they did collect the information to do it from each front. It was a far cry from the Republic's state, where Shin could send the same report for five years without anyone noticing... Except for that last Handler.

Even the news Shin was watching—or at least half listening to, as his nose was in the books, as always—probably broadcasted a more or less accurate and truthful report of the goings-on of the battlefield. The number of casualties that day was broadcasted by the government every night, with even the lowest of privates being mentioned. And the citizens would bemoan the loss of soldiers they'd never known. That was an obvious thing to do in the Federacy, it seemed. And they talked about countries that had been their neighbors until ten years ago, countries Theo had never even heard of.

But even as he thought that the Republic's white pigs really were insane, there was a part of him that couldn't sit still. Something told him he couldn't stay put like this, that he mustn't dawdle here. A burning impatience gnawed at his heart.

He couldn't stop thinking about it.

We are, after all...

Carrying his sketchbook under his armpit, Theo wasn't surprised to see there weren't many other artists out here when it was this cold. He walked around the pristine plaza, without a shred of garbage in sight, much less the debris and wreckage he was used to seeing.

Sankt Jeder had also seen its share of combat during the revolution ten years ago. Some of the flagstones were newer than others; some of the girders for the bridges over the river streaming through the city were left charred black; a magnificent, historically important cathedral was missing its belfry—likely blown off by bombing—and was left as is.

Vines crept over the cathedral's stone walls, reminding Theo of ruins he'd found on the battlefield once, despite being in a populated city. He decided to sketch the place, and the nearby priest gave him a piece of candy for some reason. He then heard a pair of quiet footsteps approach him and turned around to see Anju.

"There you are. You said something about going around the Republic Square today, so I figured…"

"Yeah, I didn't think there'd be something like this in front of the old Republic embassy, though… What's up?"

Anju was dressed in an elegant blouse, a light-colored coat, a frilly skirt, and lace-up boots. He still wasn't used to seeing her in anything but her field uniform. That applied to everyone else, too, and even himself. He was always filled with the odd feeling that this didn't suit them, that they were out of their skin.

"I want you to help me out a bit. And by that, I mean help me carry grocery bags; I just don't have enough hands for it."

"Ah, roger that… Will just the two of us be enough? Want me to call someone else?"

Kurena, who didn't have much in the way of physical strength, and Frederica, who was a child, weren't prime candidates when it came to carrying things.

"Raiden's…at his part-time job. Shin should be free, though."

That said, they all had plenty of free time on their hands. They were bored, even. As he spoke, Theo reached up to the side of his head, intending to activate his Para-RAID ear cuff.

"Activate."

But his fingers only floated through the air, instead of pressing on the ear cuff's hard texture.

"…"

Oh, that's right, Theo thought, falling silent. Anju suppressed a smile as she held out a cell phone, which prompted Theo to take out his own.

"Well gee, this thing sure is *convenient.* You gotta make sure to always have it on you—you can't connect to the other person if they've got it turned off—and you gotta manually input phone numbers to register them."

His expression and examples didn't match his first sentence in the slightest, which made Anju chuckle.

"Well, RAID Devices still had to be reset whenever we changed Handlers."

"Yeah, for the white pigs… That was annoying, too. They did whatever the hell they wanted and then complained about stupid shit every time they showed up."

The Republic had put the RAID Devices on them at its own convenience and had also attached the variable data registration ear cuffs on them in a way that meant they couldn't remove them on their own. Since they were attached to them crudely and without the use of disinfectant, when the Federacy removed them, it left scars on their bodies. Theo didn't mind it that much, but seeing how they'd marred Anju's and Kurena's beauty left him seething.

True enough, though, the Handlers in charge of them…or rather, of Shin, would end up changing rather frequently, but that wasn't particularly any fault of theirs. Their last Handler was a weakhearted little princess roughly their age, but that was on her for insisting on suffering through it and not quitting when she could.

"The Federacy sure is weird for wanting those things, though. We've been using them forever but still have no idea how they work."

"That I get. It's useful on the battlefield. The Eintagsfliege are a problem here, too. But caring about the Juggernaut, now, that's a good one. What do they think they'll get out of analyzing that walking coffin?"

When they came under the Federacy's defense, all the things they had on them were taken away. And for whatever odd reason, the Federacy decided to research the Para-RAID and the Juggernaut, so they were sent to some laboratory. All their other belongings didn't have much sentimental value, so they let the Federacy dispose of them.

"…Come to think of it, Shin asked to have his handgun back, but the Federacy turned that request down even though civilians can get approved to carry weapons."

Ernst did have it stored away, however.

"It wasn't exactly out of sentimental value, though. It was the gun he used to put the dying to rest. Shin wouldn't allow anyone else to bear that burden."

He wouldn't even let Raiden, his vice commander, who'd fought beside him the longest, do it. Theo sighed.

"I guess he wouldn't, and there's no way around that... But man, would it kill Shin to live for himself a little more?"

Theo thought their friend, who could hear the voices of wandering ghosts, was far too obsessed with the dead. Or perhaps with death itself. For instance, his fixation on the duty of putting the mortally wounded out of their misery. Or with his countless comrades, whom he swore to take with him to the very end. All those who fought and died beside him all the way from his first unit to the Spearhead squadron. And all those who were assimilated by the Legion and had their last regrets echoed by the Black Sheep. And most of all, his brother's now-avenged...but long-dead missing head.

Anju's blue eyes stared at the ground, as if she were in deep thought.

"Maybe there were some things he could only do because of that obsession, though."

"The hell does that mean?"

"Fixating yourself on a goal can also mean that there's something to *keep you grounded*. Maybe having the goal of taking out his brother is what kept Shin with us."

What if he'd been grounded by the countless whispers of the dead haunting the scar on his neck...or ironically enough, by the voice of the brother who'd inflicted that scar on him?

"We, the Eighty-Six, were meant to die on that battlefield, so we can't help but feel this way. And Shin especially had a part of him that thought of nothing but his brother. And now that he doesn't have that anymore... I'm a little worried."

"..."

That theory didn't quite hit home for Theo, but Anju was always one to observe those around her carefully. Her theory may very well have been true.

"What about you?"

"Huh?"

"We should have died back there on the battlefield, but we're still alive. Have you...decided on your future, like he said?"

Anju's lips, the color of spring flowers, broke into a bitter smile. A stray thought lingering in the back of Theo's mind floated to the forefront. *Ah, she's started wearing makeup.*

"You're seriously asking me that? It should be obvious by now."

Theo's lips parted slightly.

It should be obvious by now...

"Right."

"I thought a lot about what things would be like if Daiya was still with us, or if we had a little more time to consider our options. But then I realized it wouldn't make much of a difference. If it's a question of what we *should* do versus what we *want* to do, I think we—"

"Yeah."

Theo nodded, as if already knowing what she would say.

"I feel the same way. Heck, I think the rest of us do, too. It's all we know, after all."

It's all *we* know...

As they realized they were on the same page, a cozy, satisfying silence fell between them for a long moment. Finally, Anju clapped her hands together.

"But putting that aside."

"Oh, right. The bags."

He'd forgotten. He brought up Shin's number on his cell phone and selected AUDIO CALL. An antiquated dial tone repeated in his ears... And after it droned on for a fairly, considerably, extremely long time, Theo frowned in annoyance.

"—He's not answering!"

†

For a long time, Shin's dreams were nothing more than cruel reproductions of the night his brother killed him. He couldn't remember many dreams that didn't revolve around that. And yet, he knew that this was a dream.

"I know how selfish of a request this is."

Kaie smiled, standing in a place surrounded by white fog. A female comrade of his from the Spearhead squadron, who'd died on the battlefield of the first ward of the Republic's eastern front. She had the black hair and eyes distinctive of the Orienta. She was dressed in a desert camouflage field uniform, and her hair was tied in a ponytail.

Her small head, however, wasn't in its rightful place. It was detached, as if it had been blown away in her final moments; Kaie cradled her head in her arms, her face smiling.

"You reached your final destination. And you brought us all with you. So you should have the right to put us behind you. But..."

There were so many comrades he couldn't save, so this Kaie probably wasn't the real Kaie but rather a representation of all of them. Those who'd had their corpses stolen by the Legion or been dragged away while they were still alive and then had their neural networks assimilated. He shuddered to think of his many friends who'd been reduced to the heretical Black Sheep, hiding among the white sheep of the Legion.

"I can understand that, but it still hurts. Lingering like this hurts. I died, so I want to move on, Shin—our Reaper."

Kaie smiled as she called him by that alias. He had grown rather fond of it. Beneath her military boots were thick grassland too deep to walk in and a set of rails, divided in eight. Behind the silky gauze of the white fog, Shin could see the gray silhouettes of broken Juggernauts as well as a single Scavenger.

They were standing on the Legion-controlled battlefield of two months ago.

"Please save us."

The Black Sheep, who carried only a degraded copy of the human brain, had no personality of their own. Even the Shepherds didn't have the cognitive ability of a living human being, and mutual understanding with them was impossible.

So the girl before him wasn't the real thing, nor was she an amalgamation of his friends... Maybe she was the symbol of his regrets. The

things he'd left behind. Because at the time, the most he could do was bury his brother.

"...I will."

"Shin."

Opening his eyes upon hearing his name, Shin picked himself up from the eight-person table he had fallen asleep at in the Imperial Capital Library's reading room. Eugene was leaning his elbows—albeit not sitting—on the backrest of the chair opposite him, his silver eyes grinning at him from behind his glasses. His little sister was probably reading a picture book somewhere, but she wasn't nearby at the moment.

"I know it's warm with the sun out, but if you fall asleep, the librarians might get angry with you. It really is sunny here, though. Perfect weather."

This annex's reading room received natural lighting from a skylight. The sun's weakened rays warmed up the thick, old frosted glass, and the soft light spread throughout the room in a lace pattern. In the summertime, the elm trees planted outside would obstruct the sunlight. In the afternoon, the sunlight would warm up the room, and other boys and girls their age, sitting at the other tables, were also dozing off, halfway through their reading or studying.

"What, did you stay up late last night?"

"No, that's not it."

That hadn't happened in years. Only when great exhaustion overtook him—probably a consequence of overusing his ability—would he fall into such a deep sleep that even having someone he'd never met stand right in front of him wouldn't wake him up. Shin thought, belatedly, as if it was someone else's problem, that he must have really let his guard down.

He'd grown used to a life without the noises of the hangar and sounds of bombardment in the background. A life where he didn't have to constantly watch the movements of the nearby Legion. But he could still hear their wails echoing from the battlefield far away from here. The voices of that army of mechanical ghosts who were multiplying rather than diminishing, plaguing the earth with their haunting wails.

Eugene leaned forward, his silver eyes concealing an impish smile.

"It's almost time. You wanna go see them? It's a little-known secret, but the hall here has an observation terrace on its top floor. Not a lot of people know you can go out there, so it's a bit of a ways from here, but the view's great."

"...View of what?"

"The parade, of course. For the Holy Birthday. The western front's 24th Armored Division should be coming back, so we'll be able to see the new third-generation Vánagandrs."

"..."

Eugene tilted his head quizzically at Shin's sudden silence.

"Oh. You're not interested in Feldreß?"

"That's not it..."

If anything, he was surprised the person he was speaking to was interested in the topic. Putting aside Shin's unshakable dissonance at his Alba origins, Eugene's thin physique and kind expression looked as detached as could be from the severity of the battlefield. His fingers were a bit rough from the calluses he probably got from housework, but they weren't the kind that came from physical violence or handling weapons.

"I was just surprised *you* were interested in it."

Eugene laughed bashfully at those words.

"Yeah, I'm, uh, actually enlisting soon. Hopefully to the armored division, so I figured going to scope them out... I thought we might be the same in that regard, too."

Yesterday, Shin was at the military history shelf, and before that, he was leafing through the memoirs of renowned soldiers and war heroes. He was browsing through the same books Eugene was, so it was possible he was studying here instead of school... Maybe because he was planning to attend the same special officer academy. Eugene had developed an affinity to Shin because he thought they might be the same, so said the Alba boy with a smile. Apparently, he'd been looking for a chance to say something to Shin for a while now.

"The capital might be peaceful, but our country's at war. And who knows when the fighting might reach these streets. So I have to make sure that never happens… And besides, I want to show my sister the sea someday. So we have to end this war."

Kaie's voice in the dream echoed in his mind again.

Please save us.

The battlefield he'd left behind.

The battlefield he'd once fought on and chose to march through of his own will until the final moment. And despite making that wish, he wasn't on that battlefield anymore. He'd almost forgotten what lay beyond the Gran Mur's walls. A rotten Republic that turned its eyes away from reality and, through stagnation, decayed and lost all means to defend itself.

And the way I am right now, standing here and refusing to move forward, is the same as hiding within those walls.

"…Right."

The Legion's wails never ceased. They still moaned as they prowled far-off battlefields. Shin turned his attention to the voice of the decaying, mangled corpse of the Republic. He couldn't hear it—

Maybe because she was still alive there. Still fighting. Trying to follow in their footsteps.

"…Maybe I've rested for too long."

The words he muttered to himself were so faint they didn't reach Eugene's ears.

"Oh, I got a text. It's from Shin."

"Whaaat?! Why did he message *you*?! I tried calling him a million times!"

"Yeah… I think it's because you called him too much."

Kurena stopped halfway through her round of window shopping, pausing to look at the lively march on the other end of the street. As soon as she turned her attention to it, she stiffened at the sight of a massive silver-blue shadow that paraded through the street, cruising between the buildings. An overbearing 120 mm muzzle stuck out forward, with a long barrel and a large, clumsy fuselage. With each step of its eight legs, the tank's massive weight shook the flagstones, and the sound of the energy pack powering its propulsion system growled into the air.

Eight legs and a propulsion system...

Realizing it wasn't a Legion, Kurena released the breath she had been holding without realizing it. Her hand reflexively jumped to the tip of her shoulders, which was where the strap of her assault rifle would be if she were still in the ruined battlefields of the Eighty-Sixth Sector.

"...That nearly gave me a heart attack."

Calming down, she realized she'd seen this kind of Feldreß before on the news channel that Shin and Raiden had taken to watching. It was called a Vánagandr. It was the Federacy's primary weapon and had a cannon with the same caliber as a Löwe's, which it also matched in terms of armor. It was a far cry from the Republic's Juggernaut, which, under normal circumstances, couldn't even hope to rival a Grauwolf, much less a Löwe.

It was probably a victory parade. As a lively marching tune played, the Vánagandr advanced, the sun shining off its shiny, new coat of paint, with the Federacy soldiers marching next to it in ceremonial uniforms.

The gaze of an officer riding the Vánagandr's turret fell to Kurena, and he waved at her. Once she'd recovered from her momentary surprise, she waved back. The young officer, probably a few years older than her, flashed a smile full of pride and gave her a joking salute before disappearing along with the rest of the parade down the street.

This country was also at war with the Legion, and that Vánagandr should have been a weapon for fighting them, but somehow, it was a peaceful, awe-inspiring sight. The parade seemed bright and fun, but Kurena wasn't quite used to places packed with people. Turning around, she resumed her trip.

This peaceful lifestyle they had been granted was fun once she'd

gotten used to it. They were free of the routine tasks they'd had to per-
form every day on the battlefield, and so at first, they'd slept the days
away. But her friends each found their own ways of enjoying their new
lives, each of them gaining new acquaintances and friends. Even Kurena
had a few new friends whose names she had added to her mobile phone's
memory.

They all decided they would spend their time like this. They would
each explore this country and decide on their own future. And no matter
what decisions each of them came to, the others would respect them.

Kurena approached a shop that caught her attention, and she examined her reflection in the shop window. She was wearing a dress that
she'd found in a magazine, and it had a cape with a fake-fur trim. She
also wore a pair of boots with high heels, which she still wasn't quite
used to, but she was working on it. At first, she'd worn only the clothes
Teresa and Ernst's secretary would wear, along with clothes she'd seen
other girls her age walking around in. But lately, she had started picking
out clothes for herself.

She tried a few poses she thought were cute in front of the window's
reflection, and the shopkeeper lady gave her a thumbs-up and a smile
from inside the store. That made her happy, if a bit embarrassed. She
bowed her head apologetically and walked off.

Being able to choose your own clothes. To dress up as you'd like. To
buy whatever you wanted and walk freely. To live without thinking you
might die tomorrow or be troubled with the battle that awaited at the
end of today. It was like a dream.

…Yes.

This was a dream.

The cheering of the parade behind her died down. The silence left
in the wake of the sonorous military band's march stabbed into the blue
sky, as if to remind her that beyond that endless azure sky was a darkness
that didn't allow the existence of man.

She'd heard of this once before. Yes, back in the Eighty-Sixth Sector. It might have been Kujo. Contrary to his rough exterior, he was an
expert in astrology. Or maybe it was the female captain of the first squad

she was assigned to. Or maybe it was Shin, soon after she met him. Whoever it was, she remembered now.

The blue of the sky was only a curtain that covered boundless darkness.

The sky, the seas, the beautiful blue—they were all the outer layer of a world that meant only death for humans.

…Maybe that was why paradise was beyond the heavens.

Kurena stopped in her tracks and turned around. The march's music echoed up to the sky. As if to inform those beyond the sky that they would soon be joining them. The crowd prayed silently, the ex–service members saluted, and all the while, the Vánagandr marched on, draped in black in mourning. The number emblazoned on its turret was the number of those who'd died or gone missing on the battlefield since last year's parade. And each and every one of them had a name and life of their own.

But an even larger number of soldiers were still fighting out on the front.

This life was fun, but it was nothing more than a transient dream for Kurena and the others.

No matter how sweet the dream, we all wake up eventually.

†

"I'm back… Huh."

Raiden blinked, surprised to see the entrance hall's lights switched off as he came back from his part-time job. Whenever he came home, Teresa had the front door and entrance hall lights switched on; she said that the light should always be on to welcome them home.

Light spilled from the living room that was directly connected to the entrance hall, and he found Frederica there, sitting snugly on a large sofa, holding a stuffed bear in her arms. Shin had bought it for her a short while ago at a department store, when Frederica pestered him that she wanted to go shopping. Frederica wasn't allowed to go outside alone. She didn't attend school, either.

"Welcome back."

"Ah, thanks… The others aren't back yet? Where's Teresa?"

"She left on a shopping trip some time ago but has not returned. Perhaps something happened?"

She gave a small, forlorn sigh. And at that moment, Raiden heard a loud gurgling noise echo through the room. He fixed his gaze on Frederica, who was most likely the cause of the noise, only to find her blushing red and hugging the bear ever more tightly…before eventually saying in a delicate voice:

"Raiden… I'm hungry."

"…Huh…? Oh…"

Checking the clock on the wall, Raiden did note it was usually the time they'd be having dinner. Raiden and the others might be used to eating at sporadic times because of their former life of battle and night raids, but it was hard on a child like Frederica.

"Gimme a sec."

Raiden set down his bag and headed for the kitchen.

Unlike the Republic, which had only synthetic food both in- and outside its walls, the Federacy had fields and farms that allowed for the circulation of real food. Raiden rummaged through the refrigerator, picking ingredients to make something simple, and then washed, cut, and mixed them in a frying pan. He figured he'd make something simple to stave off Frederica's hunger until Teresa came back and prepared dinner. Frederica, meanwhile, gazed at him with sparkling eyes in the same way one might look at a wizard.

"You're proficient in the culinary arts?!"

"Eh, enough to get by."

Living long enough on a battlefield where you had to do everything by yourself forced you to pick up certain skills whether you liked it or not… Well, that was the case for *most* people. Not to name any particular exceptions to that rule…

"Next time this happens, if Shin's the only one around, and you're hungry, tell him to go buy you something. If you value your life, never let him cook for you."

Frederica's expression turned oddly happy.

"What, is Shin incapable of cooking?"

Raiden suddenly remembered a time when he used to find joy in seeing adults that were bad at certain things. Raiden shrugged, remembering those faraway days of his childhood.

"It's not that he can't. He's just too rough."

He would season ingredients unevenly, not pick out eggshells that had fallen in, overcook the soup, and so on. His creations weren't inedible…just nasty. And the worst part was that Shin didn't seem to have any desire to improve his cooking. That led to Shin being barred from kitchen duties in virtually every squadron he had ever served in.

However, for some reason, he was extremely good at handling a kitchen knife and had somehow gained a secret technique that kept him from tearing up when cutting onions. That special talent was a bit useless in the Federacy, given that food processors handled that particular duty.

Until now, Raiden and the others hadn't minded since he'd had combat and commanding to pour all his concentration into, which meant he hadn't had the time of day to give to any other skill. But the fact that nothing had changed, even in their current life as civilians, meant he was nothing more than a rough, clumsy person here.

"I see, I see. I suppose it stands to reason, considering he devoted his entire existence to eliminating his brother… Incidentally, what is it that you're making, Raiden?"

"……Have you never seen an egg before?"

He was just about to crack an egg with one hand into a bowl. That last Handler of theirs was a sheltered princess in her own right, but even she probably knew what an egg was. Though he was dubious as to whether she knew how to crack one open.

"Correct. Teresa insists that the kitchen is a maid's sovereign territory and forbids my intrusion at every turn. So eggs are sold in oddly shaped cases, I see… Do they heat them up to harden them to such solidity?"

"It's not a case, kiddo—it's a shell… Were you raised in a box?"

"Well…"

Frederica began speaking but broke off her sentence, falling silent. Raiden turned his eyes away.

Well, if she can't answer, that's that. He already had his suspicions about her background. They probably all did. But their only answer was a "So what?" and they chose to not pry any deeper.

"By the way, what were you—?"

The living room's door creaked slightly, and Shin entered the room without so much as a peep.

"…Maybe Frederica should start helping out with the cooking."

Frederica stiffened in surprise, but Raiden looked back at him calmly. Living with him for four years had made him accustomed to Shin's noiseless gait.

"If you're the one saying that, it means she's hopeless. Welcome home… That's a lot of baggage you got there."

When he'd gone out, he'd been dressed only to go out for a walk, but now he was carrying heavy grocery bags in his arms. Anju, Theo, and Teresa entered after him in succession, carrying paper bags and chilled packs, prompting Raiden to raise an eyebrow.

"…What's this all about?"

"Teresa went shopping, but her car broke down at the store. Once she was done, she had trouble carrying all the bags, and I happened to be there."

"And Anju alone wasn't enough help, so she looked for me, and I contacted Shin."

Theo lowered the chilled pack he was carrying and twisted his shoulders, as if in mild complaint.

"Next time you're doing this kind of shopping, just tell me or Shin ahead of time. We've got nothing to do. The least we could do is carry some bags."

"I would be a failure as a maid if I were to force children living in the house I'm serving to carry bags."

"You're not serving us. You're serving that weird old guy."

"It is all the same."

"No, it isn't. He's not our dad."

If Ernst were present, he would probably burst into tears and start whining. Lastly, Kurena entered the living room.

"Ah."

She stood stock-still at the living room door. Maybe it was because everyone's gaze had fixed on her, or maybe there was something she wanted to say once it was all five of them, and she didn't expect the other four to be there.

"Welcome back, Kurena."

"Ah, yeah. I'm back… Um."

She looked over at Anju, her golden, catlike eyes wavering anxiously. There was a spark of hardened resolve hidden in the depths of her eyes.

Raiden gave a small sigh.

Ah, so she's made her mind up, too.

A pair of bloodred eyes fixed on Kurena as she stood still, their usual cold calmness growing lax.

"You ready?"

Kurena nodded, his tone and words giving her the final push she needed.

"Yeah. I think I've seen everything I needed to see."

Shin had probably decided from the beginning and had simply been waiting for the others to come to their own conclusions. But they would all likely end up coming to the same decision he made. And so she said it. A smile found its way to her lips as pride filled her heart.

"Let's go back to where we belong."

✝

Having finally finished his work, Ernst returned to his estate. Hearing the children's voices, he felt relieved to see they had gotten used to life in the Federacy. If there was any positive takeaway from them having been sent to the internment camps at the age when they should have entered primary school, it was that that was the age when normal house-holds had already taught children things like basic economics and common sense. They had no trouble buying things in stores and behaving themselves in public places.

Shin and Raiden were blessed to have had guardians in their youth, and considering the environment they'd lived in, they were fairly educated. Theo, Anju, and Kurena weren't as lucky, but the fact that they could read that faulty weapon system's manual and calculate ballistic trajectories meant they were, in a way, a cut above the common Federacy civilian.

As the Empire, in its age of militaristic dictatorship, had monopolized higher education for the nobles, there were still many children who'd never gone to school or were incapable of writing their own names in the Federacy, especially in the territories. This was part of the reason why Ernst's temporary post as president, which was set to last until the Federacy would be able to hold an official election, had lasted for ten years already.

Ernst had enjoyed examining possible higher learning institutes and technical schools in between his office work. Shin loved studying, so he considered sending him to a high-class academy. Raiden was good with mechanical work, so a technical school would do well for him. And Theo... And Anju... And Kurena...

He gave considerable thought to each of their individual personalities in order to come up with good life paths for them to take, and he enjoyed doing so. It was what he wanted to do—but couldn't—with *her* child. They should go back to being normal children. Go to school. Laugh with their friends. Let them concern themselves with harmless things like aspirations, crushes, or where to hang out this weekend.

They could have a do-over for the childhood they hadn't been allowed to have, right here and now. And he had the power to make it happen for them. Was it nepotism? Yes, it certainly was. But his position should allow him these kinds of benefits, shouldn't it? His granting these children who came under his wing a happy future would surely be excused.

But there was just one single thing that bothered him. He'd given them all their own rooms and the kind of allowance an affluent home would usually give children their age. But their rooms never filled up with possessions. They would buy only what they absolutely needed and nothing more. These children had been raised to want nothing but their own well-being and the safety of their comrades. And Ernst thought that now would be a good time for them to learn the joy of wanting, gaining, and cherishing things...

And because he thought so...

...when Ernst returned to his estate for the first time in a while, he met the five children again and listened to their plans for the future. And all five wished to enlist in the military. When he heard that they wished to return to the battlefield they had finally escaped, Ernst dropped all the documents he had prepared to the floor.

"Wh-why?!"

The kids looked back at Ernst, who had yelled despite himself, with dubious expressions. He didn't have the presence of mind to feel happy that the kids felt comfortable enough around him to make those kinds of expressions.

"What do you mean, why?"

"Didn't we make it clear from the beginning? If you're letting us choose freely, we're going to enlist."

"But..."

He knew that. He'd received the report from their monitoring officers, and the children had said as much when they'd come to this estate. But he'd thought they'd said that only because they didn't know anything else. They didn't know peace. They didn't know harmony.

Even though they now knew a life where they didn't have the slur *Eighty-Six* pinned to them. Even though they could finally afford to think about the future...they still...knowingly...chose this?

Raiden gave Ernst a pained smile, in spite of the fact that he had learned to smile more gently—more honestly—since coming here...

"I'm sorry for suspecting you at first... It's a nice place you've got here. So we ended up staying here a bit longer than we thought."

"We've rested enough. We need to start moving forward again."

"So we're going back to where we belong."

To the battlefield.

Ernst shook his head slowly. He couldn't, for the life of him, see the word *so* connecting the wish to move forward with the act of returning to the battlefield.

"But why...? Why would you willingly walk back into that hell...?"

They'd fought so desperately to survive, and finally they'd escaped it—

Shin suddenly fixed his gaze on Ernst, who was as confused and concerned as if it were *his* future they were deciding. Even after tasting salvation, their intent had not changed. It wasn't even a choice they had to grapple with. This decision had come so terribly naturally to them, as if there had never been any other option. But since Ernst had been kind enough to give the time and opportunity to explore other avenues, they'd decided to try to reexamine things—

At most, they'd learned that there were certain changes they could make to improve their quality of life, but they never had any intention of growing accustomed to this place. Nor did they ever intend to stay here. This one-month grace period they'd been granted was only a brief respite from their endless struggle against the Legion. They took the month to confirm what they already knew; this place of peace was not where they were meant to be. After being isolated from peace for far too long, it did not feel nostalgic to them. Only distant.

But even if he did think that this peaceful life wasn't a bad thing in and of itself, Shin's heart remained unmoved by it. These words were the smallest kindness he could offer to the man who gave them the opportunity of a lifetime, who lamented their choice even though it had no bearing on him.

"We were just lucky."

He had the ability to hear the Legion's voices and know where they were. Their last Handler had helped them cross the Legion's patrol line, in a manner distinctly unlike the Republic. And when he had finally lost his strength on a corner of the battlefield, his brother had loaned him aid.

Luck was what had brought them to the Federacy, and their fallen comrades simply hadn't been lucky enough to enjoy similar fortune. That, and nothing else, was the only thing that set Shin and his friends apart from them.

"We just happened to be saved. And we wouldn't be able to face those who passed away if we got comfortable here and stopped moving forward. We're still alive...so our battle isn't over yet."

They'd left the plates carrying the names of their dead comrades with Fido. The plates were meant to serve as both their last offering to him and their desire to leave proof that they'd reached their final destination. But they had no intention of leaving behind those they swore to carry to the very end.

They could still remember every single one of them. They were still with them. And they promised to bring them all to what lay beyond the end of battle.

"The Legion are still active, and if we don't fight, this country won't survive. We can't turn a blind eye to that and pretend to be happy. What kind of life would we be living if we just waited idly by for the Legion to come snuff us out? We could never live like that."

If they could, it would mean they had become that which they loathed the most: the Republic of San Magnolia, the despicable white pigs. The fools who ran from the battlefield and sealed themselves in a shell of fake peace, foisting their war with the Legion onto the Eighty-Six, only to remain without a means to defend themselves in the end. The Republic, which practiced such flagrant disrespect for life that not only were its citizens unfit to be considered human, they were unfit to be considered living beings at all.

And as they ran through the Legion's territories, fully prepared to die on their Special Reconnaissance mission, they had seen the Legion's tactics firsthand countless times. Shin could hear the sounds of the Legion even now. In this very moment, he was haunted by the wails of those mechanical ghosts that multiplied endlessly.

The Republic never stood a chance. The Legion might very well consume all of humankind. Because they were painfully aware of that threat, Shin and the others couldn't turn their eyes away from it any longer.

Because they were the Eighty-Six.

Even if they were on a battlefield, surrounded by countless foes, they would fight until their lives ran out. They took pride in combat. Found purpose in it. Against all odds, they fought with everything they had, even if the only weapons left at their disposal were their own flesh and blood. This resolve was all they had left after they were abandoned by their homeland and robbed of their families.

"Even if our deaths are unavoidable, we have the right to choose how we go out. Fighting until the bitter end is the way of life we chose for ourselves. So please…don't take that away from us."

Raiden, who had only listened until now, suddenly smirked, remembering the final words Shin left to that last Handler of theirs.

"Besides…if she catches up to us after you hit her with that 'We're off' line, it'd be so awkward you'd probably never be able to live it down."

Shin didn't grace that playful remark with an answer.

But Ernst only shook his head at those words.

"That's wrong. That's, that's so wrong…!"

Ernst knew war well enough. He was once a commander for the Imperial army and later took part in the revolution as one of its leading key figures. He took many lives and left many to die, and he knew many people who bore scars similar to those of these children. Those who lamented the fact that they shamelessly survived while their brothers in arms died. He'd seen too many former soldiers racked with the sorrow and guilt that forbade them from feeling happiness while others passed away.

But that wasn't true.

"You're only here because you fought so hard to get here, so you can take pride in your accomplishments and accept this as the reward you've earned! Your fallen comrades would want this, too, if they were truly your friends… You shouldn't need to feel obliged!"

Obliged to have survived.

Obliged to have gained peace—to have gained happiness.

And unless they made that distinction, people would never escape their pasts, and they would live on, unable to feel happiness without the eternal regret that their joy was built on the sacrifice of others…!

But the five's expressions hadn't changed in the slightest. If they did understand what he meant, they weren't moved by it at all. And driven by an inexplicable unease, Ernst opened his mouth to continue but was stopped by Frederica, who had been holding her tongue until now.

"Cease this, Ernst."

Taken aback in his most unguarded moment, Ernst lowered his gaze to Frederica, who looked back up at him with cold crimson eyes.

"It is a kindness to prepare a comfortable roost for an injured bird… But to prevent it from taking flight once its wounds have healed, because you fear the world is too dangerous, means confining it to a cage. These birds have finally escaped their cage of persecution. Do you intend to lock them in a cage of pity next?"

Pursing her pale lips for a moment, Frederica spoke again—almost spitting out those words—with a wounded gaze. It was an expression a caged animal might direct toward a human looking at it from the outside.

"Surely you realize it would be no different from the Republic's conduct."

Ernst was at a loss for words.

"And for the record, these children are neither helpless nor incapable of understanding their position. Children eventually leave their parents behind. If you truly profess to be their father figure…respect their wishes and let them go."

Ernst stood quiet, silenced by the words of the young girl. And in response to those words, unbecoming of her age, Shin looked down at Frederica.

"I suppose we should be thanking you, *Your Majesty*?"

Snorting at his words, Frederica directed a fleeting gaze at him.

"...You knew."

"Vaguely."

A conduct and speech unfit for her age. A girl under the care of the president, albeit a temporary one, who did not attend school and was forbidden from going outside alone. The way she was treated was as if they were trying to keep her existence secret.

And to top it off:

"There's also something about the way you speak. I thought it sounded familiar and only remembered just a short while ago... You speak the same way my mother did."

That was what little he could remember of her. The memory of his parents' faces and voices had been washed away by the flames of war and the ghosts' incessant wailing.

"Come to think of it, your parents were of Imperial blood, were they not...? If we trace back your origins, we may well find your relatives. But if you do not wish to meet them, we can drop the matter here."

As he directed a puzzled look at her, her deep-red eyes, so much like his own, gazed back at him with surprising seriousness.

"You were abandoned by your motherland and robbed of your blood relatives. And I do realize that without a country to trace your history back to, or a race to draw your culture from, pride is the one way you have of maintaining your identity... But that way of life is much too flawed. Three things make a man: the homeland he was born into, the blood running through his veins, and the bonds he forms. If you have none of those and try to preserve your soul with naught but your pride, you will eventually lose your sense of self and crumble into nothing... Hear my words and commit them to heart."

"..."

Those words felt oddly real to Shin and were surely not something he would have expected to hear from a girl not even ten years old. It was as if she was recounting the events of someone she had seen fall into ruin. As if this was an answer she had come to after a long, arduous struggle with a question. A sense of déjà vu nudged at his heart. Those bloodred eyes, so much like his own, looking up at him. They wavered for a moment before she closed them tightly and looked up at him again with surprising resolve.

"Know my name, for it is Augusta Frederica Adel-Adler. The last empress of the great Empire of Giad, the very people who commanded the Legion to conquer the continent... I am to blame for the loss of your homes and families. Condemn me for it, if you must. I welcome it."

Raiden parted his lips to speak.

"How old were you back then?"

The Legion's invasion started ten years ago. This meant Frederica, who was turning ten this year, was only a baby back then. And they did hear that for its final two hundred years, the Imperial royal family was reduced to puppets under the control of the high nobility, who ran the dictatorship.

"The Republic pigs were the ones who took everything away from us. We wouldn't mistake them for anyone else... Don't underestimate us."

"Forgive me."

The girl hung her head in shame. But after shivering once, she raised her head again.

"In acknowledgment of that pride of yours, I have a request to make of you, Eighty-Six... If you are to return to the battlefield, take me with you and aid me in vanquishing the ghost of my knight, who roams the battlefront still."

There was no need for Frederica to explain any further. Not to them, the Eighty-Six, who couldn't afford the luxury of burying their dead comrades and, at times, even saw their corpses being dragged away.

"The Legion took him."

Frederica gave a small nod.

"He was the Legion that attacked you shortly before you reached the Federacy. He bombarded you in the middle of battle... You referred to it as a Shepherd, I believe?"

"How can you tell that's him?"

Shin was able to tell one Legion from another because of his ability. But there was no way for the Federacy, which didn't have the Sensory

Resonance technology, to single out a specific Legion unit. Nor was there any way a girl living in the capital could tell that a unit she had never even seen, hiding in the battlefield, was her knight.

But Frederica replied to his question with a pained expression.

"The ability passed down by my heritage allows me to peer into the past and present of those I know… Forgive me. The wound your brother inflicted on you…must have been painful."

…Your neck… What happened…?

Frederica had probably seen everything back then. His past, when his brother nearly killed him. And the moment when he shot down the Dinosauria possessed by his brother's ghost. And the moment he swore he would do it at all costs, when he was the same age as her…

"I can do naught but see. I lack the strength to save my knight, who calls to me from the battlefield. So please, I ask for your help. Just as you saved your brother… Please save my knight."

Shin finally understood the déjà vu Frederica made him feel. She reminded him of himself at the moment he decided to save his brother, who had died in a corner of the battlefield, when he was just her age.

"—I will."

Ernst sighed heavily.

"…Fine. I'll arrange for Frederica to be enrolled in your squadron as a Mascot… But I have only one condition I insist on."

Six apathetic gazes fixed on Ernst, dissatisfied with him apparently making things harder for them.

"You will enlist as officers. To be specific, the Federacy has a special officer academy, so you will enlist through there. Otherwise, I won't allow it."

It was necessary to finish one's secondary education to join the academy, and some in the group hadn't, but it shouldn't be a problem. The Federacy's war situation wasn't good enough to pay much heed to these kinds of details.

Kurena, however, narrowed her eyes dubiously.

"Huh? What's the point of that? It doesn't matter how we enlist or what rank we are."

"Regardless. I am your guardian, and you are under my responsibility. Your parents surely would have wanted this for you, and I can't act against that."

"You don't know that—"

"I do… I was a father once, too."

He, too, was once the kind of person who wished for the joy of his children from the bottom of his heart.

"Former officers have a wider range of options compared to former soldiers. I want you to have as many paths open to you as possible once this war ends."

Once this war ends.

Those words left the children with expressions of surprise. The war with the Legion had raged on for as long as they could remember, and their lives were dominated by its madness. Their expressions told him it was a prospect they had never once considered.

Ernst thought those words were probably cruel to them. For five years…five long years they had fought. And perhaps even before that, when they learned their families, who went off to fight, would never return. They had hardened their resolves ever since then. They waited for their parents, who wouldn't return, and watched as others died in the war, not knowing whether tomorrow held the same fate for them. And even if it didn't come the next day, there was no escaping fate—

They would surely die.

If nothing else, they chose to live and die as human beings. And he wished for these children who fought fate, armed with nothing but that resolve, to survive. He hoped they would live long, fulfilling lives without fear of a predestined death. He prayed that these children—who could only live in the moment—would carry out a way of life that was opposite that.

And they probably didn't realize just how cruel of a wish that was.

"This war will surely end one day, and if you intend to see it through to the end…you would do well to consider what you'll do when it does."

CHAPTER 4

BENEATH THE TWO-HEADED EAGLE

The 177th Armored Division's headquarters' large conference room was dimmed, with only the holo-screen's light illuminating the faces of the gathered unit commanders. The Eintagsfliege's jamming, blocking all efforts to observe the depths of the Legion's contested zones, was as true for this room as it was for anywhere else in the Federacy, but the Federacy's military wasn't so incompetent as to neglect its reconnaissance duties.

There was something to be gained even from what fragments of information they could pick up. Fluctuations in the traffic. Noise signatures picked up by the self-propelled, unmanned reconnaissance probes, their numbers and bearing. The reports of the recon squads that ventured into the contested zones, risking life and limb.

"—In accordance with our findings, the integrated-analysis team has surmised that there is a high probability that the Legion are preparing to launch a large-scale offensive within the coming days."

The major general in charge of the 177th Armored Division, seated in a leather chair at the back of the room, sighed at this report.

"We'd figured as much, and yet… The time is finally upon us."

They had predicted the Legion would eventually stage an offensive to break through each of their fronts.

A shadow suddenly rose from the darkness. A young female officer—her blond hair cut short, her eyes a shade of purple, and her red lips smeared with refined rouge. Officers died one after another in the Federacy's military, which sent them frequently out into the field, and yet, the rank insignia of lieutenant colonel—unusual for her age—glinted off her collar, and she wore the research division's armband and a pilot's medal on her chest.

"What is it, Lieutenant Colonel Wenzel?"

"Major General, sir. I'm sure the 177th Division will reorganize in preparation for this large-scale offensive. I would like to ask that you release my squadron on this occasion."

The conference room buzzed with doubtful whispers. The air filled with a needlelike enmity, and the major general sighed as the beautiful woman before him beamed with a fierce confidence.

"The Reginleif is still in its testing stages. Whether or not they can withstand deployment on their own is still unknown, and as such, we will continue deploying them along with Vánagandrs."

"But if I may, sir, the Nordlicht squadron holds the highest number of downed hostiles not just within the 177th Division, but within the 8th Army Corps as a whole. I believe this achievement stands as sufficient justification for their individual deployment."

"And their number of casualties is equally high… I'm afraid a Feldreß that had half its forces killed in action upon its first deployment is simply not trustworthy."

"Think of it as a sort of screening process. The rate of casualties since then has been decidedly low."

A voice from somewhere in the conference room cut into her words.

"That's a shameless enough thing to say, given that you're relying on the Eighty-Six's experience… Only a rehabilitated weapons dealer like you would ever send those poor children into battle again."

The voice was steeped with far too much indignity for it to be banter, and the woman's expression froze for a moment. Her eyes wavered, as if holding some emotion in them, but she restrained it the next moment and opened her mouth to speak again.

"My XM2 Reginleif's mobility far surpasses the Legion's, and depending on the strategy employed, its combat capabilities are in no way lower than theirs, either… If we are to prepare to intercept the Legion's large-scale offensive when they far exceed our numbers, the group strategies we're employing right now will not be effective. As such, we should go against conventional strategies and employ groups of select elites in few-versus-many combat."

Having finished her statement, the beautiful woman flashed a softer smile. Her purple eyes were fixed on the major general before her. The commanding officer narrowed his eyes as he returned her gaze. She was his junior in the military staff college, and he could tell what this woman was thinking even without her having to say it.

Cut the bullshit and just say yes already, you stupid drone beetle.
Goddamn spider woman.

"In the name of the safety of our Federacy and its civilians, do properly consider how to best utilize my Reginleifs and the Nordlicht squadron, Major General, sir."

†

The Legion's forces successfully pushed into the second defensive line the following night but were pushed back by a counteroffensive staged by the Federacy army.

"—That's fine and all, but can't you do something about how they're treating us…? They send us appeals for reinforcements left and right, but once they're done with us, they just dump us into a hangar or a warehouse. Do they think we're dogs or something?"

"I think the bases just aren't equipped to accommodate us. Those are special reinforcements appeals, you know?"

They were sitting in a corner of a spare hangar that FOB 13 had provided for them as lodging. Raiden sat on a canvas that served as a makeshift bed, and Shin answered his question, sitting nearby on a substitute chair.

It was an early army morning. The sounds of this advance base's personnel clamoring and the combatants getting ready to set out could be heard from outside the hangar. The base was coming alive, but they—who weren't part of this base—didn't have anything to do.

The Nordlicht squadron would usually be stationed at the rear division's headquarters. But having been sent out to act as mobile defense personnel, they were in a somewhat peculiar position, as the base didn't have a headquarters building for the rear forces.

To be specific, any base that sent appeals for reinforcements was in charge of providing them with supplies and lodging for their next sortie, and they were to operate from that base until they were summoned elsewhere. Those appeals were on a platoon—and not a squadron—level, and so the squadron was scattered across different bases. This had been their situation ever since they were assigned to Nordlicht.

Fortunately enough, advance bases would often welcome troops that weren't assigned to them, depending on the results of battle, and had no shortage of makeshift beds and rations. The base did provide them with some lodging in the residential block, but that was allotted to their female members, Frederica included.

"The Reginleif is still considered to be in temporary trial usage, so they might not be willing to outfit them for us. I wouldn't be surprised if they don't have the leisure to do it anyway."

"Yeah, we got hit hard yesterday, after all… So according to your predictions, they should be coming soon, right?"

Shin shrugged at Raiden's fleeting glance. The ability his brother had cursed him with remained active, even after he'd achieved his goal and defeated him, and still alerted him to the state of the army of ghosts. The situation wasn't simple enough to sum up with "coming soon."

"It's more like they could attack at any moment… They've been ready for a long while now."

But the base's morning clatter drowned out the ghosts' commotion, and it felt somewhat far away to Shin.

"—Our squad only ended up losing two members, Fabio and Beata from the second platoon. It wasn't even such a dangerous situation, but an infantry unit was attacked by Grauwolf types, and there were some friends of theirs in there, so they rushed to defend it."

They were walking through the residential block's hallway, their footsteps squeaking against the floor. The Nordlicht squadron, which had no headquarters on the front lines, of course had no office for the squad's captain or his vice captain to use. As such, Bernholdt followed half a step behind Shin, simply giving the report he normally would have delivered in the office on the go instead.

"This reduces the squadron to twenty. We've sent a request to have new members sent in, but the normal armored division got hit considerably hard, so I doubt they'll have anyone to spare for us. We do technically belong to the research bureau and are a gathering of mercs... Plus, our head honcho is a weirdo even by military and research-bureau standards."

Lieutenant Colonel Grethe Wenzel, commanding officer of the 1,028th Trial Unit. They'd seen her once, when they were appointed, but they hadn't actually spoken to her.

"I'd bet people don't think too highly of her, seeing as she developed the Juggernaut."

"It's the famous pilot killer that sent ten people to the hospital when it was only in its testing stages, after all. And she's an heir to a long-running family of military-industrial-complex owners. Thanks to that, we have plenty of spare parts and rigs, but people like to call her an arms dealer for a reason."

Shin replied to Bernholdt's words in an indifferent manner.

"We're used to not getting resupplied, be it equipment or man power. But it's good so long as we still get spare parts."

"I've already told you this, but the Republic was messed up for doing that. Please don't judge us by your Eighty-Six standards of good and bad."

Nonetheless, when Bernholdt had heard Shin was an Eighty-Six, he'd seemed mostly convinced. At the time, the Nordlicht squadron had only enough personnel to make up a battalion and had a regular army captain serving as its leader. He hadn't been very capable, to put it mildly, and his lacking command had led to the death of many squad members, himself included.

The fact that Shin, who had been only the vice captain of a platoon at the time, had ended up taking over the role of captain was seen as an act of desperation. A green recruit straight out of the special officer program couldn't fill this role.

But be that as it may...

"...You'd have had it easy in a standard armored unit. Why'd you come to such a wreck of a unit?"

"It's easier for me here. A normal unit's chain of command and combat regulations make it hard to move."

When he was piloting the Republic's "drones," there were no combat regulations to uphold and no commanding officers to breathe down his neck—with the exception of their last one. He was too used to moving by his own judgment and taking responsibility for his own actions, and the Federacy's standard military's method of abiding by a commander's judgment and obeying orders wasn't one he could get behind.

Bernholdt scoffed.

"I can't believe I'm hearing 'it's hard to move' from a damn teenager... Well, I guess we're not complaining so long as your orders don't get us killed. Even if you are a stone-faced reaper and a snot-nosed brat who keeps rushing to the front despite being the commander and literally driving us insane with that noise if we Resonate with you."

Ignoring the sarcasm steeped into Bernholdt's words, Shin turned his gaze to the window. Outside, an open-top truck stood there on the paved road, surrounded by clouds of dust. In its trunk were black body bags, piled on top of one another like sacks of potatoes. Those were probably the remains of the soldiers who'd died yesterday.

The thought came to mind, suddenly, that Eugene had probably been collected by now. He'd been his contemporary, who'd said he fought for his family.

I could ask you the same thing.

Shin knew what Eugene was going to ask, but...how would he have answered if Eugene had asked him back then?

"Second Lieutenant? Second Lieutenant... Are you listening?"

Shin came to, realizing Bernholdt was looking at him dubiously.

"Ah, yeah. Sorry."

"Yeah, well, I guess I can understand. You brats actually sleep at night, and fighting through the night's starting to get to you... But that's, er, a bit of a problem, though," Bernholdt said abruptly.

He stopped walking and looked ahead, visibly dumbfounded. Adjusting his gaze to match Bernholdt's, Shin realized exactly what was bothering him. His eyes fell on the sight of Frederica, who was apparently suffering from lack of sleep. About several nights' worth. She was waddling around barefoot in her pajamas, dragging her stuffed bear with one hand, and her hair was a mess.

Although it was a clear violation of army regulations, Bernholdt was originally a Vargus who put very little emphasis on discipline, and Shin, who originally piloted a drone, didn't care at all. But she was wearing a blouse in place of pajamas, and its three top buttons were open. It was sliding off her right side, exposing her thin shoulders all the way down to her chest. She may have been ten years old, but it was still a problematic sight.

"Frederica, either go back to your room and change or go back to bed."

"Uuuh. Kiri, comb my hair..."

Shin sighed once.

"*Frederica.*"

Her red eyes blinked once and then opened wide.

"Shinei... Pardon. I mistook you for..."

She gave him a proper response but kept on walking, which prompted Shin to grab her by the scruff of her neck. Anju had fortunately just come out, so Shin decided to let her handle things.

"Sorry, Anju. Could you handle this?"

"What's wrong...? Ah, Frederica?! Look at yourself! Come here, quickly! Theo, can you go get Frederica's uniform?"

"You're dropping this on me? Aaah, fine."

Theo, who happened to be passing by, changed directions and walked toward Frederica's room. Watching him retreat, Bernholdt opened his mouth to speak.

"What was I saying, again...? Ah, right. We got another 'package.' HQ contacted us about it the other day."

"Package...? Oh..."

Realizing what Bernholdt meant, Shin sighed. Six months or so

after being rescued by the Federacy, they began receiving letters and goodwill packages from "well-intentioned civilians." Even though Shin and the others weren't small children, some included plush toys and picture books and letters filled with excessive emotion. Ernst didn't disclose their personal information, so the Eighty-Six would be able to live peacefully in the Federacy. But that only cemented their image as "poor children who were persecuted by the terrible Republic."

It didn't matter much to Shin what people thought about him, and he didn't care whether he was the subject of selfish goodwill and pity, but being made into a spectacle didn't sit well with him.

"You can dispose of it all, as always… And having to deal with this every single time is annoying, so could you tell HQ to just get rid of them every time?"

"Inspecting 'em every single time is as much a bother to them, and they feel bad for you being the subject of cheap sympathy, so the boys at HQ would love to do that. But some people would make a fuss over embezzlement and criminal negligence, so they still want me to let you know."

Looking back at him, the young sergeant who was nearly twice his age shrugged.

"It's all about formality, Second Lieutenant. An army is an organization made up of people, after all. And since people are irrational and inefficient, the army is full of irrational and inefficient procedures."

And well, that was at least originally true in the Republic as well. That reminded him of a certain voice, as clear as a silver bell. At first, he'd found it annoying, as the owner of the voice would pester him about filling out his combat reports and sending out his patrol reports, but…

Bernholdt's hoarse voice snapped him out of his thoughts.

"And that's about it. That concludes my report, Captain. Please sign this document."

Shin heaved a sigh.

"So…"

As they had breakfast, Theo feigned a foul mood.

"Don't you think sending someone to bring your clothes, then calling him an 'insolent fool' the second he opens the door, is cruel and unusual treatment? She even threw her stuffed toy at me. And if that wasn't enough, she started hitting me afterward."

Theo summed up the events that had happened after he'd gone to get Frederica's uniform at Anju's request. And while he didn't actually care much, he still made it out to be a big deal so he could keep teasing Frederica about it. Anju, who had witnessed the whole matter unfold, covered her mouth to hide her lips twitching up into a smirk. Raiden and Kurena were more astounded than amused, and Shin was, as always, stoic and apathetic.

Even though they were all part of different platoons in the Nordlicht squadron, this was the first time in a while the five of them had gathered. As they were in charge of mobile defense, they were continually sent out to battle. The western front's defenses were pressing enough that the Federacy had no qualms about working a trial unit—that focused on implementing a new, suspicious weapon system without many achievements under its belt—to the bone.

Frederica hung her head, a blush creeping over her face.

"We fixed your blouse, but for some reason, you took it off again."

"You weren't so much half-awake as you were still in dreamland. If you were that tired, you could have just gone back to sleep."

"Aaaah, silence! Be quiet, I say!"

The girl brushed them aside, failing to notice the casual consideration behind Theo's words.

"To be clear, it is your fault for not knocking and walking in on a lady as she was in the middle of changing her attire! Don't you agree, Kurena?!"

"He did knock. Also, you're no lady."

"Why did you take off your pajamas before he came back with your clothes anyway?"

"The biggest problem is that you were streaking around the hallway half-asleep and half-naked, Frederica."

"I did no such thing! And who told you about that?! You weren't present to see it, Raiden!"

The answer was obvious. Everyone's gaze fixed on Shin, but the boy himself proceeded to ignore this. Frederica fell to her knees.

"...I never knew you could be so malicious..."

"All I said was that if you can't be expected to put on your clothes or hold a conversation properly, we can't expect you to join us on sorties. It might be better to send you back to HQ."

Frederica pursed her lips in displeasure. As Shin met her red eyes, which were looking up at him grumpily, he continued.

"You can't force military regulations on a Mascot, and you have no obligation to join us when we sortie. I won't call you useless, but if we can't guarantee your safety, we'd be better off if you went back to the rear."

"I cannot do that... I have come here to see things through to their conclusion."

Raiden smirked.

"So I hope starting tomorrow you won't be streaking around half-asleep."

"Can't you put that matter to rest?!"

Frederica howled at him, her face turning red again. The five of them decided to drop the subject, as teasing her any further would just make them feel guilty.

"Well, then. I guess our itinerary is mostly cleanup duty."

Once battles end, soldiers on the front lines have plenty of work cut out for them. Repairing, maintaining, and rebuilding defensive positions. Recovering the wreckage of downed enemy and friendly units. And of course, recovering the corpses of dead soldiers. They may have pushed back the enemy offense, but the 177th Armored Division took massive losses. In all likelihood, every place they'd go would likely be understaffed.

"It's either that or patrolling the contested zones... The armored units got done in hard in yesterday's fight, so it'll probably be patrols."

"I know we can't say we won't do it because there's no need for it here, in a standard army. But having to patrol when we know there's no point in doing it is kind of annoying."

"On the other hand, Anju..."

"I know..."

Snapping shut a schedule book with an illustration of an adorable cartoon character on the cover, Frederica sighed in a tone unbefitting a young child.

"Everyone's been working you to the bone, and yet, you have grown so accustomed to it. However..."

Everyone gazed at Frederica apathetically. While Shin and the others were in the special officer academy, Frederica had already been enlisted in the trial unit and had actively taken on the role of coordinator between the squad's captain and the research bureau.

"Grethe has summoned you. As such, we will be returning to headquarters today."

The 177th Armored Division's headquarters' base was built on an old Imperial air force base, which granted it an abundance of hangars and maintenance stations, as well as large runways that were currently only good for receiving transports from within the country. One such hangar had a barracks attached, with one of its rooms turned into a control room. This served as the 1,028th Trial Unit's headquarters.

"—Before we begin, I would like to thank you all for your fine work in your constant reinforcement missions."

The 1,028th Trial Unit's commanding officer, Lieutenant Colonel Grethe Wenzel, welcomed them with her rouged lips curved in a smile. They were in a briefing room with a glass window overlooking the hangar, located one floor below the HQ room. The people in charge of the research section and maintenance section were gathered there, along with the squad captain and all the other Processors—in other words, Shin and the other Eighty-Six.

Looking over the combat unit's commanders, who lowered the room's average age by quite a bit, Grethe smiled wryly.

"Our roster has changed since you took on your new post last month... It would seem the Reginleifs were most compatible with the Eighty-Six and the mercenaries."

Twenty of her "creations" were lined up behind the soundproof glass, receiving thorough inspections and maintenance after having returned to their usual roost for the first time in a while. The first high-maneuverability Feldreß in Federacy history, the Reginleif. It put emphasis on speed, with the concept of "maneuverability that does not give the enemy the chance to lock on." It was the manifestation of Grethe's ideals and extensive theorycrafting.

The Vánagandr was powerful with its 120 mm cannon, but if it got hit anywhere other than the turret, it would be destroyed all the same. In that case, forgoing armor and focusing on speed should ensure the pilot's safety. A month ago, this hangar was filled with the impressive sight of a battalion of fifty brand-new Reginleifs.

But now the wreckage of these creations lay in a despondent heap along with vast quantities of containers of 88 mm shells, leaving a conspicuous void where the others once stood. Less than half the units remained, and their pilots were these young officers, still in their teens. And yet, it was too soon to pass judgment. Far too soon...

"Before we go into directives, I have some good news. The other day, we confirmed the survival of the United Kingdom of Roa Gracia and the Alliance of Wald. One of our patrol units picked up a wireless sound signal."

Those were respectively the last autocratic monarchy to the north of the Republic and the Federacy (the Empire at the time) and the armed neutrality nation that neighbored them to the south. With the Legion's jamming, it had been impossible to ascertain their survival, much less communicate with them, but now they knew both of them at the very least seemed to still be intact.

"It appears they've both managed to somehow erect a defensive line and maintain enough space to survive. The United Kingdom seems to be gradually advancing to the south, so we should soon be able to send people over there. We may yet be able to begin collaborative strategies with them. However, we are still unable to get in touch with any of the other neighboring countries or the Republic of San Magnolia..."

She stole a glance in the Processors' direction, smiling wryly at Theo, who hung his head with his cheek pressed against the table, and Kurena, who lowered her gaze apathetically. They neither worried for the Republic as their homeland nor reviled it for persecuting them. They were completely and utterly indifferent about it.

And that only made Grethe realize how deep the wound ran. Shin and Raiden listened carefully, but they seemed worried about something—or perhaps some*one*—else. Anju turned her gaze to them, perhaps thinking the same thing.

The maintenance-team leader, a man with a mane of red hair streaked with gray, opened his mouth to speak.

"So I'm assuming the directives are going to be bad news, Lieutenant Colonel?"

She nodded at his jesting question.

"I'm afraid so… We've received predictions that the Legion may be preparing for a large-scale offensive in the near future."

The research-team leader, the only civilian in the room, gasped. And at the same time, the platoon leaders, who'd seemed bored until now, gave her their complete attention. Grethe didn't like the metaphor, but it was like seeing dogs rise from their sleep in a doghouse at the sound of a hunting horn.

"In accordance with this prediction, the western front's army will be reorganized to maximize its fighting potential. The 1,028th Trial Unit will be attached to FOB 15 as an armored squadron. We will be subordinate to the 151st Regiment, and I will be assuming direct command… You will not be divided into platoons and passed around different units any longer. We will concentrate all your strength into a single squadron. The time has come to show the Reginleif's, and the Nordlicht squadron's, true worth. Any questions?"

"—What scale will the offensive be?"

The reorganization and change of their assignment was either something Shin had assumed would happen or something he didn't care about. Grethe smiled at Shin's indifferent words.

"We're predicted to be capable of pushing it back with our current forces. We will have reinforcements prepared in case the worst happens… Which reminds me. I've received the report you submitted regarding this situation, Second Lieutenant Nouzen."

Raiden sneaked a glance in Shin's direction. Shin completely ignored the gaze coming from his side, which was something Grethe caught on to. She didn't know what it meant, though, and decided to let it slide.

"I found it quite fascinating. Both your analysis as a field commander and your opinion as the captain of an elite unit in the Republic are quite valuable. But still, you only have the perspective of a battlefield under the jurisdiction of one division. Don't you think predicting a large-scale offensive of the entire western front was a bit too daring?"

Shin's reply came immediately, as if he'd predicted this would be her retort.

"Had the 177th's sector not been a unique battlefield, even within the western front, I would not have had enough material to make such a conjecture... During the last battle, it felt to me as if the Legion pulled back. Like they had no choice but to pull back."

They weren't pushed back. Nor were they lured out. Grethe's smile suddenly vanished.

"The more territory we take back, the longer and thinner the front line becomes. You probably still haven't finished building the fortifications and frontline bases from when you made progress three months ago... This situation doesn't strike me as a favorable one."

"...You're sharp. You know, you'd be cuter if you acted your age a little more."

Shin didn't even twitch an eyebrow at her jest. Grethe sighed.

"Your words have merit, Second Lieutenant. And HQ acknowledges that. But if we're simply content with maintaining a defensive line, the Federacy will eventually fall. The Legion won't disappear if we simply wait. We have to advance, even if little by little, and exterminate them as we do."

"..."

"And if the Legion's aim is to draw us out so they can stage an all-out attack, your prediction assumes their numbers are simply too great. Far beyond what the integrated-analysis room estimates."

It even exceeded the theoretical limit of the Weisel's presumed output. It was the kind of number that would put the western front's defenses in a state of utter inferiority, even if you added all possible reinforcements.

Looking at the reports submitted by this usually taciturn boy made it clear that, given his environment, he had a staggering amount of knowledge and cleverness. Perhaps it was his long service in the Republic. Maybe being forced to fight the Legion in such a defective weapon system instilled in him a tendency to overanalyze the enemy.

That seemed to align perfectly with his penchant for ignoring orders and strategies if need be and acting on his own accord (which was something Grethe was covering up for him, in light of his achievements)... But that served to prove that the Republic had inflicted deep wounds on him as well.

"You've nothing to worry about... The Federacy is not the Republic. We would never think that turning our cheek from the threat in front of us would make it go away. We've put effort into gathering information and performing thorough analyses and are making whatever preparations we'll need. And more than anything, the Federacy will never abandon a brother-in-arms."

You don't have to fight alone and unassisted, like you did on the Republic's battlefield. You won't have to fight a lonely war in a state of utter inferiority, without information or support, ever again.

"..."

Without seeming convinced, but also without stirring whatsoever, he closed his bloodred eyes. Grethe smiled as she watched him. It was probably still too soon to earn his trust or respect.

"Furthermore, new members will be joining the squadron. I will be introducing them, so please try to maintain cordial relations with them."

Having been instructed to follow her, Shin and his group followed Grethe down the hallway as her high-heeled shoes clicked loudly against the floor with every step. Only Shin and the other Eighty-Six followed her; they'd bidden farewell to the familiar maintenance-team leader and the research-team leader, who was always dumbfounded at their odd conduct during inspections.

"What's your opinion on the Reginleif, Second Lieutenant? Do you like it better than that aluminum coffin of yours?"

Grethe smiled deeply as Shin stared back at her.

"I was in the base that took custody of you back then, too. I was in charge of counterintelligence and disease control, so we never got to speak… But I have your old partner in my lab. Want to see it?"

"…No, thank you."

He had changed units frequently since he often wrecked his rig beyond repair, so he hadn't actually piloted it all that long. And besides, it was an old unit of his—a partner that was defeated and finally allowed to be laid to rest. Shin didn't want to do something that would equate to digging up its grave.

"…I believe I've been submitting my reports on it and the Para-RAID in time."

The 1,028th Trial Unit was established in order to test the Juggernaut and the Para-RAID technologies. One of his duties was to submit periodic reports on them and their influence on the human body.

"Yes. But I want to hear your opinion—as someone who piloted a Feldreß of a similar system in the Republic."

Shin sighed once.

"If you're asking about the Juggernaut—"

Grethe cocked an eyebrow.

"It's called the Reginleif."

"Juggernaut."

"Re-gin-leif."

"Juggernaut."

"…Whatever. Well?"

Grethe shook her head in displeasure, and Raiden coughed awkwardly in an attempt to stifle his laughter. Shin ignored them both and continued:

"It's an aluminum coffin that's made much better than the Republic's."

Grethe fell into a full ten seconds of silence, unsure whether she should take offense.

"…Really?"

"What, she hasn't noticed?"

"What he's saying is that it's nothing more than a pilot killer."

Grethe was probably too shocked to hear Kurena's and Theo's whispers. The Reginleif's maneuverability was too high for ordinary people to pilot. It was, after all, developed with the explicit intent of giving it a mobility that matched the Legion's, so safety apparently wasn't a factor.

And as a result, its Operators all retired during the test stages, having sustained injuries all over their bodies. And when it was deployed into real combat, it devoured any ordinary Processor that piloted it. Shin, Raiden, and the others managed to pilot it only because they were Eighty-Six. During their childhood and into their adolescence, they were forced to pilot the Juggernaut, which was also built without regard for the safety of its pilots, and their bodies matured so as to adapt to that strain.

"That's a very…shocking impression. That weak…or rather, brittle… failure of a Feldreß, that makes me question the sanity of the person who made it…"

This wasn't something one would usually say in front of the Processors, but Shin didn't mind. It was the sad truth, after all.

"…How on earth did you ever fight in that wreck of a Feldreß back in the Republic?!"

"That's all we had."

"Yes, that's right…"

She seemed to mumble something inaudible. Probably cursing the Republic and its arsenal.

"…I don't think it's a bad rig. It may pick its Processors, but its speed is a boon. And for how fast it is, it brakes well, so it's got some flexible maneuverability. The Vánagandr's as much of a metal coffin, after all. The Juggernaut's still preferable to that one."

The Republic-made Juggernaut's thin defenses were mostly there for peace of mind, and the Eighty-Six didn't place much trust in armor. This new Juggernaut, which was developed with mobility that wouldn't allow it to get hit to begin with, was, in their eyes, preferable to the slow, armor-reliant Vánagandr.

"I see… For some reason, that doesn't feel like a compliment."

"…He wasn't trying to compliment you…"

Grethe seemed to ignore Anju's jibe. Sighing heavily, she said:

"And you chose to become Processors despite this?"

"I've heard you were the one who asked to have us Eighty-Six added as prospective Operators, Lieutenant Colonel."

"As test personnel and nothing else. I didn't think you'd volunteer to join the combat unit. And while it's true your experience and skills have been a great help to us...I was honestly opposed to sending young soldiers to the front lines. Much less you, the Eighty-Six."

Grethe shrugged at Shin's gaze.

"I was an Operator, too. Ten years ago, when the war with the Legion first began. I was just about your age... A young flight cadet, but the Legion stole the sky away from us."

The Anti-Aircraft Mobile Cannon type, Stachelschwein, and the Eintagsfliege's jamming still held the Republic's and the Federacy's aerial superiority in check to this day.

"I volunteered along with other cadets... Many of us died. They surrounded us while that blasted Vánagandr moved at a damn crawl. I kept thinking over and over: What if we had a faster Feldreß? That's what led me to develop the Reginleif."

Having lowered her gaze in recollection, Grethe looked up and smiled faintly.

"...I appreciate your honest opinion, Second Lieutenant. The rest of you, too... I'll try to improve it for our next retrofit, so I look forward to a more favorable opinion, okay?"

Crossing the base's gate, they paced down a newly paved asphalt road. Even after that road ended, they kept walking, entering the summer grasslands. Shin's eyes stopped when he noticed a familiar set of rusted rails, divided in eight, under the grass.

"Last time you all came through here, this place was still under Legion control."

Grethe turned toward them, her red lips curved in a proud smile.

"But over the last six months, we've managed to reclaim our land, pushing back as far as here."

Shin could hear someone heave a sigh behind him.

*   *   *

In the middle of the summer grasslands, surrounded by white flowers, five Republic mobile weapons—four Juggernauts and a lone Scavenger—lay enshrined in a casket of glass.

"We found them when our front line expanded. I know you may think it unpleasant, but we had to run some inspections on them. The same holds true for the names on the monument... We put the plates back where they were after we finished recording the names on them. You can rest easy."

Grethe laid a hand on the solemn stone monument beside the glass case. It was built in the Federacy's style, which Shin recognized from the military graveyard he visited once before.

"I don't know how the Republic sees it, but the Federacy considers those who fell in defense of their country as heroes to be revered. And that's why the names of the fallen are preserved on monuments in the military graveyards... But since they were your companions, we decided to leave them here, in this place you reached. This is where they belong, and this is where they'll stay."

"..."

They didn't really want this, Shin thought dryly. Neither he nor they wanted to be forever memorialized through this kind of pretty little monument. All he wanted was for someone he knew to remember him, even if just for a moment...

...I wonder if the major still remembers us.

That was all he'd wished for on that night, when flowers of flames bloomed in the sky.

"...Second Lieutenant?"

"It's nothing."

He shook his head lightly.

It seemed the people of the Federacy saw things differently from them in this regard. He didn't expect to be understood... But still, he was a bit grateful for their attempt to be considerate. And with this monument, or even a single document that listed their names, these plates were no longer needed to prove his comrades existed.

Shin turned his gaze to Fido's remains sealed in the glass case, thinking that this was one long-term mission he'd ordered the Scavenger to complete.

May you carry out your duty until you crumble into dust.

The Legion had their own units to collect wreckage, the Tausend-füßler. Fido was to keep watch until it was eaten away by one of those or until the rain and wind made it crumble away. All it had to do was last even a bit after they used up what little strength they had left...

He could hear familiar footsteps approaching and stopping behind him, the four legs making a clattering sound as it paused. Shin turned around, only for his gaze to fall on the giant form of another Scavenger, standing there silently. It had a squarish body, four short legs, and two mechanical arms. It was an old type, the kind you hardly even saw anymore in the Republic's Sectors.

Another sound of footsteps, this time of a pair of small army boots rushing toward him, belonging to Frederica, who was running his way, cutting by Raiden's side.

"Hey! While your impatience is relatable, there was no need to run so quickly that I fell off, was there?!"

Frederica stood there gasping with her hands on her knees, and Kurena reached for her long hair from the side, brushing off leaves, petals, and various bugs that clung to it.

"Where have you been, Frederica?"

She'd shown up to inform them about the meeting but was gone before Shin noticed.

"I—I was off at the laboratory...overseeing this one's...activation. Grethe and the researchers...had been working on this...'surprise' for a while now."

"Surprise?"

"Wait, did you just run here all the way from the lab? Are you okay? You're not dying, are you?"

"I...rode this one...most of the way here. But as soon as it saw you...it accelerated, and I fell off."

"Catch your breath first, Frederica. You can tell us everything afterward."

"...So what's the deal with this thing?"

After taking a moment to calm her breathing, Frederica took a step back proudly.

"I'm glad you asked, Raiden! This is…"

"—Fido?"

Shin whispered, cutting into her words, or rather, having not listened to her at all. Raiden eyed him wearily.

"Don't tell me you're gonna start calling all your pets Fido now."

"That's not what I mean…"

Frederica smiled with satisfaction.

"I was sure *you* would notice. But you are correct—this is indeed the same Fido that fought alongside you in the past."

There was a moment of silence—

"""""Huh?!"""""

—followed by four voices overlapping in one exclamation of shock.

Looking up at Fido, Shin's eyes were uncharacteristically wide with surprise as he was frozen in place.

"When we inspected the grave markers you left, we also took the chance to analyze this one. Its interface was ruined beyond repair, but the core unit had somehow remained intact. That allowed us to replicate it. Oh, we upped its machine performance to an extent that it could provide adequate support, so you can look forward to it being a much more reliable ally the next time you sortie."

Frederica added that it still looked as clumsy as it ever did, as a sort of humorous quirk of the research-team leader who'd put its frame together. He realized that if they'd left it behind with their prized partner units and the memories of their lost comrades, this machine must have been a faithful attendant to them. So he believed that leaving its appearance as is would make them happy.

"This one did think itself to be 'dead,' however. Even when we put it into a new frame, it would not boot up, initially. It only started moving when…"

Frederica suddenly smiled bitterly.

"…when it heard your name, Shinei… It truly adores you."

Was that a hint of jealousy in her voice? Shin, at least, didn't notice. To be honest, he had stopped listening to Frederica's words shortly after she began speaking. He walked up to Fido, who stood still before him. He stopped an arm's length away.

"...*Pi.*"

The Scavenger's optical sensor swerved to him, looking at him timidly. Shin sighed lightly.

"I thought I ordered you to carry out your duty until you crumbled to dust. What about your mission?"

"*Pi...*"

Seeing Fido hang its head shamefully (its optical sensor and the whole of its frame leaned forward, lending it that appearance) made a small smile play over Shin's lips. The fuselage of this large metal unit no longer had any of its old scars, and yet.

"Still... I'm happy to see you again."

"*Pi*—"

It seemed even trash-collecting machines got overwhelmed with emotion at times. Fido's optical sensor flickered, as if welling up with tears.

"*Pi...!*"

In a gesture that was probably equivalent to a human being clinging to someone in an embrace, Fido rushed its body—all ten heavy tons of its weight—toward his master. Predicting the Scavenger would do so, Shin stepped aside, avoiding it just in time. Fido kept on rushing, crushing the grass beneath it as it was thrown forward by momentum, before crashing into the wreckage of a Löwe with a magnificent, comical gong sound.

"Well, can't say I didn't see that coming."

"Shouldn't you be more concerned?!"

Frederica alone seemed to be panicking.

"Eh, don't worry—Fido won't break that easily."

"I meant Shinei, you fool! He may have avoided it, but he could have died just then!"

"Shin somehow always knows how Fido's going to move."

He didn't know, or much care, whether it was the result of five years of battle together or the fact that Fido gradually learned to move in accordance to him. Shin smiled, thinking it was probably both, as he watched Fido wobble back to him dejectedly.

FRIENDLY UNIT

Autonomous Support Unit

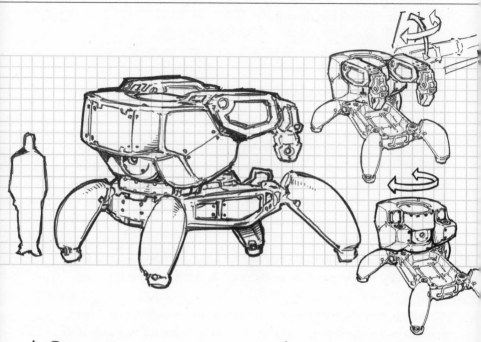

Scavenger

[SPECS]

[Manufacturer and official name]
Republic Version: Manufacturer: Republic
Military Industries [RMI] / M101 Barrett
Federacy Version: Manufacturer: WHM /
Scavenger
Total Length: 3.1 m / Height: 2.5 m
Equipment: High-Operation Crane Arm ×2
Large Container Mount ×1

A support unit developed by the
Republic to assist the Juggernaut.
On top of being in charge of supplying
spare ammunition and energy packs, it
also has the role of collecting unused
materials from abandoned or crashed
units, as implied by its name. It is
equipped with a simple AI system,
and while its normal role is to fulfill
the routine work detailed above,
Fido, the unit that served Shin and
the Spearhead squadron, has gained
impressive learning capabilities by
surviving many battles and is capable
of understanding their words. It has
taken on the extra duty of collecting
the articles of those killed in action
and has gained cognitive faculties that
go beyond those of a mere machine.

*   *   *

Grethe watched the whole affair with a smile of relief.

Thank goodness.

"…You finally smiled, Second Lieutenant."

†

The Nordlicht squadron's Processors were given rooms in the 177th Armored Division's headquarters' barracks, but due to how they were assigned, they spent most of their time performing reinforcement duties for assorted frontline bases and, as such, hadn't been in them for a while.

Shin was lying down in his relatively unfamiliar, small, modest room, totally absorbed in a philosophy book, when a reserved knock on the door roused him. They were allowed to do as they pleased between dinnertime and lights out. The sound of the hangar didn't reach the barracks, but the sound of soldiers making merry in the cafeteria was the same as it had been in the barracks back in the Eighty-Sixth Sector.

He opened the door to find Frederica. Her expression was tense, and she let out a surprised breath.

"…Tch, when will you do away with that habit of walking without making audible footsteps…?! It is bad for my heart!"

But habits weren't something you could change just by wanting to, and Frederica knew full well that Shin had no intention of changing his ways.

"How do you even silence your footsteps while wearing military boots, to begin with…? There was nary a creak from the floor just now!"

"I'm not really trying to do it."

On that subject, Daiya, Kaie, and Kino would always say he was creepy because he sometimes just showed up behind them like an actual reaper. Frederica nodded in understanding as he moved aside to allow her to enter. Sitting down on his hard bed, she looked around the bare, unadorned, almost prison-cell-like room with a frown.

"Such a dreary residence… Put up a picture or a painting or at least some books you enjoy for decoration. The decor is far too bleak."

"It's just a place to sleep. Having lots of stuff just makes cleaning up more of a chore."

He wasn't reading because he enjoyed it that much, to begin with. It just allowed him to keep his mind off other things—for example, the incessant voices of the ghosts. He had put up a makeshift shelf in his room back when he was in the Spearhead squadron, but that was just because he couldn't be bothered to put them back in the library he found in the ruins. And in the year or so since the Federacy had found them, Shin had remained as disinterested and unconcerned with his surroundings as ever.

Frederica frowned, as if she had seen through him.

"This is more than just a place to sleep in, fool. This is a place you can return to. Even if it is naught but temporary lodging… You should not leave it empty."

She sighed, saying it might have been acceptable in the Eighty-Sixth Sector. The Eighty-Six of that land could have died any day.

"Eugene's room was full of pictures, I'll have you know."

"You cleaned it out?"

"There is no shortage of places that need more helping hands. I merely helped sort through his personal articles… It was all pictures of his younger sister. His parents left no pictures behind, so he probably cherished his last family member all the more."

"…"

When Shin thought of Eugene's photos making their way back to his younger sister, his heart throbbed with a faint pain. He recalled seeing her once, in the capital's library. A little girl, younger than even Frederica. Shin was eternally parted from his parents and brother at roughly that age, and even though the countless days of battle that followed were to blame for it, he hardly remembered them. The thought that Eugene, who'd fought for his sister's happiness and died thinking of her, would go on to be forgotten by her…was a somewhat miserable one.

"…Maybe you shouldn't have asked for his name."

Frederica's ability wouldn't work on people whose names she didn't know. Only once she spoke to someone and asked for their name would her *eyes* let her see their past and present. If Frederica hadn't spoken to Eugene that morning, she would not have had to see him die on that very same day.

"That isn't the case for you and your fallen comrades, is it? I am the same. Even if death parts me from another…I prefer to have met them than to have never known them at all. I can still hold them in my memory, after all."

Shin blinked once, slowly.

"You'd be a lot better off not having fallen comrades, if you can help it."

Shin had known loss after loss. At first it was his family, and once he'd been sent out to the battlefield, his comrades were killed off, one after another. Those words were his honest, true feelings. He never regretted the oath he made with his first companions. And he had decided to carry his fallen comrades with him ever since.

But that's not to say he didn't feel pain every time he lost someone… And this girl carried the weight of her knight becoming a ghost. She shouldn't have to endure any more suffering.

But Frederica only scoffed.

"Are you really one to talk? …Kindhearted Reaper?"

"Anyway, what did you come here for?"

Surely she didn't come here just to criticize his sense of interior design. Blinking in surprise, Frederica seemed to have remembered what she came to do, and her eyes began to dart about nervously.

"Well, you see, the matter is…"

After a long moment of hesitation, she mumbled on, still refusing to look directly at him.

"…Forgive me…for this morning. Mm…"

Ah. Shin nodded plainly. *This morning, huh?*

Come to think of it, she never did tell us the name of her knight.

Kiri.

"Am I really that similar to him?"

"I wouldn't say you're mirror images. But your physiques are identical. You do draw half of your blood from his clan, after all."

Frederica smiled mischievously at Shin—who was taken aback by her revelation—like a child who had pulled off a successful prank.

"My knight, Kiriya Nouzen, is a descendant of the Nouzen clan, just as you are... Has your father not told you of your genealogy?"

"No."

No one had ever told Shin anything like that. And even if his father had said anything to that effect, he couldn't remember it.

"These are your roots, whether you are aware of them or not. You should be interested in them... The Nouzens were a warrior clan of Onyxes dating back to the dawn of the Empire. Their bloodline excelled at combat, and they served as guardians of the emperor for generations... Those of noble birth were born with unique powers and skills, and some descendants of these old nobles still exhibit such powers on rare occasions. It is the desire to preserve these abilities that made the nobles abhor mixing their blood with other races... That was likely why your parents left for the Republic, Shinei."

But hearing this did not stir any particular emotions in Shin, after all. Neither his parents' genealogy, which tied him to the Federacy, nor the circumstances that led them to move to the Republic. He couldn't remember any of that— *No.*

It's all your fault.

Whenever he tried to recall his past, that was the only memory that came to mind. Even if he knew it wasn't his fault.

Mom dying, that I'm going to die—all of it—it's all because of your sin!

Frederica had sunk into her own reminiscence and didn't notice how Shin had stiffened.

"Kiri was not a direct descendant of the Nouzen patriarchy and wasn't closely related to you. He was four years your senior... When I last laid eyes on him, he was roughly your age."

The revolution had occurred shortly after her coronation, and having been driven out of the palace, Frederica hid in a remote fortress with the rest of the dictator faction and the royal guards for as long as she could remember. It was the last stronghold of the Imperials: Rosenfort, where the blood of the barbarians was spilled during the dawn of the Empire's rule.

In a fortress full of adults, Kiriya, despite being ten years older, was closest to her in age and was her sole playmate. He would comb her hair, pick flowers for her from the garden, and follow her every whim without so much as a frown.

With the memory in her eyes telling as much, Frederica suddenly chuckled.

"But that one, too, had an overtly serious, unbending nature. The kind Raiden would surely call a stick in the mud... If you two were to meet, Shinei, I'm sure you would be very much at odds."

That having been said in jest, Shinei scoffed. He had no way of knowing the personality of this knight he had never met, but from what he'd heard so far:

"Yeah, he doesn't sound like the type I'd get along with."

"I can imagine it vividly. He would pester you to look up from your books when people speak to you or to obey military regulations and conduct, and you would ignore it altogether, which would just anger him further... Such a wistful sight."

Frederica smiled faintly, envisioning those two boys speaking, who despite the blood that tied them together never met each other alive or even learned each other's names.

"He once told me...that he wished he could meet his relatives in the Republic."

The patriarch of the Nouzen clan never officially pardoned his son for fleeing the Empire, but Kiriya believed he did. When he learned that his grandchildren had been born, he'd secretly sent them a certain picture book. And he never truly threw away the letters his son sent him. When Kiriya told her this, his hands were shaking despite his smile.

During the fighting at the start of the revolution, Kiriya's family was killed. So were his friends from other noble families. But in actuality, Kiriya's father, Sir Nouzen, was on bad terms with the dictatorship and gave up his rights quickly to join the civilians' side, and even after the

Republic's founding, the clan still maintained its status and was allowed to live. But that was something Frederica learned only after coming under Ernst's protection.

Kiriya, who'd been trapped in a distant fortress, surrounded and isolated by the civilian army, had no way of knowing that. He'd wanted to meet the rest of the clan and make them his family. Being alone was far too painful.

"..."

Shin couldn't comprehend that feeling. He'd lost his family. Even the memories of them were vague, and he had no place to call his homeland. But he didn't think having no one to depend on and living by your own strength was inconvenient. For the Eighty-Six, who made that their way of life, needing someone else to help you maintain a grasp on your sense of self was something they couldn't understand.

"How did he become a Legion?"

Frederica fell silent for a moment.

"...Rosenfort's defensive line was a fierce battlefield. The Federacy army thought that by capturing us, they could shut down the Legion."

True enough, the prime minister and the royal guards had had the authority to command the Legion and had sent them to guard their defensive position. But the Legion, who were developed as weapons of annihilation that couldn't take prisoners or tell civilians apart from soldiers, didn't have the capacity to understand complicated orders. The fact that there were many situations that required deploying the royal guards with the Legion, coupled with the fact that deploying man power with the Legion was forbidden, led to the death of many a royal guard in battle.

And Kiriya, who was the youngest royal guard and Frederica's personal knight, was sent out to battle often. And true to the blood of what was once considered the greatest warrior clan of the Empire, he killed many of the Federacy's soldiers.

"And before long, Kiriya's sanity began to slip."

He'd lost his family and friends to the revolution, and the homeland he grew up in was now enemy territory. His fellow royal guards gradually fell in battle, and the sword of their offensive was being slowly chipped away. Kiriya had probably lost too much...

Defending Frederica became everything to him, and he devoted his entire being to fighting for her safety. He would often smile at Frederica, standing beside a bloodstained Feldreß after snuffing the lives of Federacy soldiers. His smile was always so sunny and calm.

Princess.

"And the sight of that smile…frightened me."

That was why Frederica fled the fortress.

She fled—and was soon captured by the Federacy army. The fact that Ernst happened to be on that battlefield was sheer luck. They professed the death of the empress, hanging her red-and-black mantle as proof.

And Kiriya saw that. The power to know the past and present of those she knew alerted Frederica to the fact that he saw it. It happened when the fortress was consequently conquered, and the Federacy's forces pulled back to the ruins of the garrison. The soldiers who captured her were injured. As such, her mantle was dirtied with blood. Having fought and fought to save his mistress, the then-sixteen-year-old boy saw that bloodstained mantle.

Frederica's power couldn't discern what Kiriya thought at the time. But a Tausendfüßler happened to be prowling nearby, creeping about in search of matter to recycle for their war effort. Unlike the Republic's Scavengers, the Tausendfüßler weren't forbidden from collecting corpses, and they'd long since learned they could assimilate the biological neural networks of humans and use them as central processors.

And so the giant steel centipede closed in on Kiriya, seeking to claim this wondrous "prize"… And Kiriya, who stood stock-still, didn't flee.

"It was I who made Kiriya into that monster."

Shin didn't know what kind of "Kiriya" Frederica was looking at right now. He couldn't see the same things she did. The Federacy's Sensory Resonance allowed users to share only the sense of hearing. But he'd encountered the Long-Range Artillery type twice and knew its lethal ferocity. It was only natural—painful as it was—that Frederica, who'd once cherished him, would call what he became a *monster*.

"You've said the Legion will soon be upon us… Kiri will probably come then. And when he does…"

"I know."

He responded to the girl's insistent pleas with a wry smile. But the only smile she could offer in response was a sad one.

"You do not... When he does arrive, do not place yourself at risk and avoid him if you must."

Frederica averted her gaze from his.

"I may have forgotten that people perish ever so easily. As desperately as they may strive for the future."

Just like Eugene had died yesterday.

"...It is as you said earlier. I loathe to touch on the death of others—on the death of those I know. If you or Raiden or any of the others were to die just so I could put Kiri out of his misery, the scales would remain forever unbalanced. You all have futures ahead of you, and you must not lose them."

Futures.

"A future, huh..."

Frederica's expression turned astonished and somewhat worried.

"You really haven't given the future much thought, have you...? I do not much appreciate the comparison, but you should take a leaf out of Eugene's book. Consider where you would like to go on your next leave, or some such fancy. Even a minor thought like that would be fine. But just...consider it."

"..."

Have you put any thought into what you'll do once you're discharged?

For a second, he thought he could hear that silver bell of a voice again. It was shortly after Kujo died, before they knew each other's names or even felt a need to know them.

Anywhere you'd like to go? Anything you'd like to see?

At the time, he'd thought the question to be nothing more than bothersome. He'd cut the idea down, saying he'd never thought of it, and that answer remained unchanged even now. But if he'd have asked her the same question, how would she have responded? What did she feel, in that Republic that forgot how to do battle? What did she think, and did she try to fight on, as a Handler...?

*   *   *

Night came early in the battlefield.

War was a machine that consumed massive amounts of labor and supplies every day to sustain itself. The supply division and, indeed, the Federacy itself had no spare energy to supply, and turning on lights on the dark battlefield could make one a target for bombardment. With the exception of the bare minimum of posts that required light, most of the base was in a state of blackout. This held true for both the Federacy's western front and the eighty-five Sectors.

"Shin, have you seen Frederica? Ah."

It was a bit before lights out. Frederica hadn't come back, and Kurena sent Raiden to look for her. Knocking on the open door to Shin's room, he stood still. It was a small, cramped room, like a coffin or a cell, furnished only by a single desk and a bed. Shin was on the bed, reclining against a pillow as he had in another barracks Raiden could remember, caught up in his thoughts. And next to him was Frederica, sleeping as she entrusted her full weight to him, leaning against him.

"Heh, so that's where she was. She sure does like you, *Big Brother*."

"…She just sees someone else in me."

There was an odd pause before he said that. Apparently, being called a big brother rubbed him the wrong way. Raiden then remembered there was once someone like that for Shin, too. It was something Raiden, who had neither an older nor a younger sibling, couldn't help but think was inconsequential.

"Ah, right, that knight of hers… But aren't you doing the same? Seeing someone else in her."

He saw her like their fellow Eighty-Six…and like their last Handler, though that was a different sort of pity. Those words made Shin sink into contemplation.

"Yeah… Maybe I am… Because she's the same as I was back then."

"Is she?"

Confronted by those red eyes, Raiden tapped his fingertips against his own neck. The girl's neck wasn't visible over the collar of her uniform, but her knight never left a scar on her neck. As if to say that Shin's brother, who inflicted that scar on him, was completely gone by now.

Raiden then activated his Para-RAID, informing Kurena that he'd found Frederica, and shut it off after asking her to come get her. Before long, Kurena walked into the room and after shouting a brief "What are you doing here?!" picked up Frederica like a piece of luggage and walked away.

Seeing them off, Raiden pulled the desk's chair and sat on it without asking for permission. Shin's RAID Device was thrown haphazardly on the desk. Apparently, he didn't pick up earlier because he was lying down.

"...So you submitted a report, did you?"

Shin probably hadn't forgotten how Raiden had warned him about revealing his ability when they'd just arrived in the Federacy.

"I figured I would tell them what I could. The more fighting power we have, the better."

"Cut that out. There's no point in telling them because no one believes you until they hear it for themselves. You're the one who said that, remember? And even if they do believe you, who knows what that'll cause? All it takes is for someone to Resonate with you once in battle... You haven't forgotten what happens then, have you, Reaper?"

Back when they were in the Republic, no one who Resonated with Shin and heard the ghosts' wails ever connected again, with the exception of their last Handler. They all loathed Shin as a reaper. The other Eighty-Six Processors withstood it, but that was because seeing their comrades suffer gruesome deaths was an everyday routine for them. They were used to screams of pain.

But among them, quite a few shirked Shin's presence, and those who couldn't endure Resonating with him ended up dead. They would disconnect from the Sensory Resonance and forfeit the protection of the Reaper, the one with the power to overlook the Legion's battlefield. And many hated Shin for this.

And once it knew the circumstances, would this Federacy be able to accept Shin's ability to hear the voices of every single Legion? Raiden didn't think it would. It didn't stop using the Juggernaut, despite its tendency to kill untrained pilots, and continued examining the effects of the Para-RAID in what was essentially human experimentation. The Federacy was coldhearted enough to do that.

"The Federacy ain't as lofty as it might think it is, and when all's said and done, we Eighty-Six aren't equal to the Federacy's natives… For all we know, everything would be the same no matter where we went."

Pity and scorn weren't much different in terms of being looked down upon, and one-sided sympathy was nothing but forfeiting the will to understand the other side. There was no telling when one who offered goodwill would show their true colors, flipping over to reveal stark hatred. No telling when someone might call him a monster. And even if they decided he was useful despite that…

"The Legion aren't the only ones capable of picking apart people's brains. You're welcome to become their guinea pig if you want, but I ain't getting dragged into it and becoming a hostage for them to dangle over your head. Don't fuck this up."

Those weren't his real feelings, of course. But he knew Shin would care more about the people around him getting involved than his own well-being. Shin closed his eyes faintly and sighed.

"…Sorry."

"Telling them as much as you did should be enough… It's up to the Federacy if they want to believe you or not."

It wasn't a bad country. They didn't want to see it destroyed. But they and their comrades had no obligation to defend it to the death. That was all. And Shin wasn't the kind of person to avoid making those kinds of cold judgment calls.

"Are you all right?"

"…What do you mean?"

"I'm asking if you're thinking of something pointless… Did Ernst's words actually get to you?"

Silence.

"Frederica told me to consider it… Not that I ever have before. I've never needed to."

He would either die fighting his brother or perish in the Special Reconnaissance mission. Those should have been the only outcomes available to him. The very fact that he was still alive went beyond any possible future he had seen for himself. So thinking of what came next was an especially daunting task.

Raiden shrugged when asked how he felt about it.

"I think it'll work out, one way or another. Got no clue as to what I'll do, and I kinda doubt the war will even end. But working at something so I can earn enough to eat... That's easier than fighting the Legion, at least."

He may not have thought of it, either, but Raiden didn't think it was that hard a question. Working to stay alive just because you didn't want to die was probably the same everywhere, be it in the battlefields of the Eighty-Sixth Sector or some unknown future where the war ends. And putting their all into living until the final moment was the Eighty-Six's way of life, and this didn't clash with that idea.

But...

Raiden pondered, gazing at Shin's downcast red eyes. The near-decapitation scar, the proof of the terrible atrocity his brother had inflicted on him, was barely visible behind the collar of his uniform. Even after he gunned down his brother's ghost, Shin was still haunted—as if by a curse. People *like him* were different from Raiden. They needed something more to stay alive. *Something* to restrain or maybe counteract the curse.

At the edge of his vision, he saw something lying haphazardly in the room. A ridiculous philosophy book on the corner of his bed, with a piece of paper closed into it, serving as a bookmark.

If they were in the Republic's first ward's barracks, now would be when their last Handler would Resonate with them. What was she thinking right now? Or rather...

...what was she waiting for?

"...Do you think the major's doing well?"

Sparing Raiden a fleeting look, Shin shrugged silently.

Raiden sighed heavily. *Be a little honest with yourself, man...*

CHAPTER 5

CRIES "TAKE AIM"

Riding on the electronic waves, a machine's words ran through the airwaves of the battlefield.

```
<No Face to first area network>
<Commence sweeping operation>

<All Legion connected to aforementioned net-
work are to disengage standby mode>
<I repeat, commence sweeping operation>
<Targets: eastern battlefront, the Federal
Republic of Giad>
<Northern battlefront, the United Kingdom of
Roa Gracia>
<Southern battlefront, the Alliance of Wald>
<Western battlefront, the Republic of San
Magnolia>
<Directive to all Legion in the aforementioned
network>
<Commence extermination at once>
```

†

On that same day, at the same time...

...to the west of the Federal Republic of Giad, in the 177th Armored Division's Nordlicht squadron's barracks...

...a single officer jumped out of bed.

†

Raiden dreamed he was falling off a cliff.

"Get up."

His head smacked against the mattress just as he heard those words. Rubbing his neck, which hurt somewhat, as he'd slept in an awkward position, Raiden clambered off the hard bed. His small room in the barracks was dark, illuminated only by moonlight, and Shin stood there, holding the pillow he'd snatched off the bed in one hand.

"Listen... Would it kill you to *say something* before you—?"

"Now's not the time."

He responded curtly, his voice steeped with tension. And judging from how he was dressed in the Federacy's steel-blue flight suit in the middle of the night... Raiden's eyes narrowed.

"...They're coming."

"Yeah."

Looking outside the window, they could see the Eintagsfliege's silver clouds brewing on the horizon, snuffing out even the darkness of the night.

"How many hostiles?"

"I don't want to calculate it. It's like the seven seals of Revelation have been broken."

"...Did you expect me to get that reference?"

Shin using any kind of humor was proof of how bad things were. His red eyes were still fixed on the other side of the battlefield in cold scrutiny.

"...I predicted this, but it's pretty much the worst possible scenario. Part of the forces I thought would get assigned to attacking the other three countries are headed for the Federacy instead. Looks like the western front is a point of maximum importance for the Legion."

"Gee, what an honor."

Raiden rose to his feet as he grumbled sarcastically but frowned again when he saw Shin's profile illuminated by the moonlight.

"...Are you okay, man?"

"...I wouldn't increase the Para-RAID's sync rate above the bare minimum today if I were you."

He didn't try to pretend nothing was wrong. Even this stone-faced Reaper realized there was no hiding it. His red eyes laughed bitterly. His face was pallid, and not just because of the moonlight's illumination. He was pale, and his face was contorted as if he was enduring immense and constant pain.

"Don't Resonate with me unless you have to... I thought I was used to this, but tonight really is a bit too much."

The Reaper, who hadn't even batted an eye at the thunderous bellow of his brother's long-pursued ghost, was shaken.

"...Roger."

"I need you to handle preparations for our departure. Go wake the others up."

"What about you?"

Shin turned a backward glance to him and tapped the handgun on his side holster gently. It wasn't the small pistol Feldreß pilots were given for self-termination purposes. It was a larger caliber, the automatic pistol he'd used in the Republic.

"Now's not the time to stay silent. I'll go wake up the rest of the army."

While abnormal circumstances were to be expected in the army, the Processors were still fairly irritated at being woken up from their sleep. And it wasn't an official order, either, but an arbitrary decision by their captain. Even if his skills matched his title of Reaper, his coming to this decision without any alarms blaring or the area radar giving a notice left them annoyed.

"Shit, if this is a drill...I swear to God—next battle, my gun might *accidentally* fire at that stone-faced Reaper..."

"You won't have to; I'll shoot him on the spot if that's the case. Stray bullet, of course."

After the maintenance crew were ordered to prepare the Juggernauts for takeoff as quickly as possible, the hangar was filled with their thick voices and the roar of the gantry crane's engine and the heavy machinery carrying energy packs and shells. Passing near the disgruntled Processors who voiced their complaints behind the curtain of noise, Bernholdt scoffed at them.

"You can try, but he'll just turn the tables on ya. Which one of you was it that picked a fight with the captain and got beaten to a pulp instead?"

That was before everyone knew Shin was an Eighty-Six. His appearance told of his thick, noble Imperial blood, so quite a few of them took him lightly as a dainty noble and were beaten up badly when they tried to raise a hand to him.

"But, Sergeant."

"Besides, you lot were never under his direct command, so you don't realize it yet, but when it comes to the movements of those damn hunks of metal, the captain knows better than the radar ever does."

A siren began blaring. The shouting and noise died out for one long moment, and an ominous alarm rang. The alarm that warned of the Legion's invasion.

Bernholdt shrugged at the other Processors' astonished expressions.

"...See?"

In one corner of the first defensive line, the armored troops swallowed spit nervously in their trenches and pillboxes as they awaited the enemy's arrival. It was a sector that sadly wasn't blessed with the forests and ruins that made up the majority of the western front's battlefields. Still, this was a well-fortified position for pushing back the Legion's advance, and it was calculated to be within range for covering artillery fire.

In order to dampen the bombardment's deadly shock waves, the trenches were dug in precise right angles, with a thick anti-tank minefield and an 88 mm anti-tank gun set in the formation's rear. Fortunately, the alarm blaring earlier than it should have allowed an armored unit that was set up nearby to rush to the site, and its presence relieved some of the fear that the looming threat of death inflicted on the soldiers.

"...Sir."

A soldier clad in a full-body reinforced-armor exoskeleton pointed ahead. Something plowed through the night, a surrealistic, inorganic, ferocious silhouette the color of steel, pushing away even the darkness in its path. And in the next moment, their field of vision, the entire mountain range that made up the horizon, turned the color of cold steel.

"Wha—?!"

It was like witnessing the moment a tidal wave rose. The countless shadows crossed the ridges, like the instant the sea parted and the destructive wave rushed down upon them, washing the dark fields over with the color of metal. Just like a surge of water crashing down, like fire consuming a field, this proverbial sea roared with the faint, distinctive sound of that engine—of bones rubbing against one another. And even as more and more Legion formed the vanguard, their numbers continued streaming in without end, standing as bloodcurdling evidence of how vast their forces were.

The shadow spilled around them, as far as the eye could see, without a battle cry, as if the darkness itself threatened to consume them.

These were all...

"Legion..."

I am Legion, for we are many.

A thunderous roar. The shrill sound of bombardment whistled from above, signaling the descent of an iron blow from the heavens. Few present probably recognized that this bombardment of a Long-Range Gunner type served as the opening shot of this battle. That was how unbelievable this sight was—awe-inspiring to the point of being a near-religious spectacle, like the judgment day described in holy scripture.

The first bombardment greatly missed the Federacy's defensive line, landing far behind them. The second one landed far closer, this time in front of them. Those weren't accidental shots. The standard Skorpion tactic was to remain hidden several kilometers away, beyond the horizon, and shoot them from afar. The first few shells were fired to adjust their sights, and once that was done, the obvious next step was—

"Heavy bombardment incomiiiing!"

A deafening noise roared in their ears. A volley of highly explosive rounds painted the silver sky black and then rained down onto the trenches, bursting on impact. Propelled by the 155 mm shells' shock waves, the bombardment's fragments turned into high-speed bullets of incredible mass, ripping through the trenches and the flesh of the armored soldiers within them.

And then another impact came. And another. And yet another. The explosives rained down by the dozens—nay, by the hundreds—injuring or killing half the people within a forty-five-meter radius. The bombardment fell endlessly like a shower, drowning out the screams and death throes of the soldiers.

And as the soldiers remained pinned down, the steel-colored surge drew ever closer. Standing muzzle to muzzle in an orderly fashion, a massive army of Dinosauria maintained an armored wedge formation. Knowing no fear, they rushed in even under the Skorpion fire, crushing any and all obstacles under the weight of their one-hundred-ton armor.

Noticing a party of Ameise was deployed at the vanguard, the armored soldiers shivered in terror as they realized what came next. The bombardment was meant to sweep away the minefield and open the way for the Legion vanguard. The Ameise crossed into the charred earth that was blown to pieces along with the mines. A few untriggered mines were set off, blowing several units away, but the Dinosauria advanced, stepping over the wreckage.

The strategically inferior Ameise sacrificed themselves to the mines to defend the tactically valuable Dinosauria. It was the heartlessly logical kind of sacrifice only a machine would ever commit to and a human would rarely be able to go through with. And having crossed the minefield unscathed, the metallic beasts had finally made it to the trenches where what few armored infantry who'd survived the bombardment hid.

"Dammit... Defend! Defend to your last breath! Don't let them through even if it's the last thing you dooooooooooooo!"

*   *   *

The siren woke up not only the common soldiers, noncommissioned, and low-ranking officers but also the field officers and generals in charge of command. They were all at their posts, at the very least dressed in their uniforms.

Despite the electronic jamming killing their radar, a reconnaissance probe that had, oddly enough, strayed far from its normal range detected the Legion's approach, but none of the officers had the leisure to investigate why it had gone as far as it had. The probe was destroyed soon after discovering the enemy, but they launched other units in its place, and when they received the transmission regarding the observed number of troops and the calculated total sum and formation of the enemy force, everyone went pale.

"Impossible... The western front is under a large-scale attack...?!"

Grethe moaned, looking up at the Legion's estimated distribution projected on the 1,028th Trial Unit's headquarters' main screen. The 177th Armored Division's sector was on display, and on top of it was the 8th Army Corps's zone, and above them was the entire western front; they were all colored in red. The enemy units, presented in red blips, filled the monitor with such numbers that it made her weak in the knees, and by contrast, the blue blips signifying the first defensive line's friendly units were despairingly few and far between.

They had predicted a large-scale offensive would happen. They had prepared for it. But this scale and these numbers were far beyond anything they could have predicted. Considering the current state of the first defensive line, they wouldn't be able to push the Legion back, no matter how frantically they tried.

Of course, the mobile defense unit stationed at the back was preparing to sortie, but it was doubtful the front lines would be able to buy the time needed for them to complete their preparations. The fact that all aspects of their functionality were crippled by their immense weight and required the use of special machinery was the armored corps's biggest flaw. And if they couldn't maintain the front lines, their immediate response unit, which was still in the middle of preparations, would not have the time to sortie...!

A voice crackled from her commander's headset, informing her of a message from military command to all high-ranking commanders. The United Kingdom of Roa Gracia and the Alliance of Wald were also being hit by a large-scale offensive. They seemed to be doing what they could to push back, but it was unknown whether they would be capable of resisting for long.

Could this possibly be the day of humankind's reckoning...?!

"Lieutenant Colonel."

"Second Lieutenant Nouzen. What's your status? When can you sortie?"

"Ready whenever you are. The Nordlicht squadron is prepped and ready to head out."

Grethe looked into the holo-screen's inscription of SOUND ONLY with stunned silence. The control crew was equally shocked.

"We received no order to do so but made preparations anyway. I'll accept any form of rebuke later."

Taking this kind of independent action called for punishment, not rebuking, but Shin spoke in an exceedingly composed tone. He either was confident he wouldn't be punished for this or didn't care. Grethe's red lips curled upward. She never neglected to paint them with lipstick, lest her subordinates see her without it. But it seemed that time wasn't upon her yet.

"I'll cover for you no matter how much those stubborn geezers complain, Second Lieutenant... I'll have the other units launch as soon as they're ready. Hold the line until then, at all costs."

"Roger."

The Empire having been a militant country before it became the Federacy, many of the cities built during the old Empire's time were designed like fortresses to halt enemy invasions. The roads were designed to prevent an enemy from easily reaching the city center and to allow only a certain degree of width. Cities were built over rivers to divide them into areas. Houses were built in such a way that their masonry linked up with old, dilapidated walls to impede progress.

Those were, however, tactics meant for war against fellow men.

"Take cover, quickly! The tanks are coming!"

A group of armored infantry scattered the streets, making their way through the bends and turns of the paved road. The troops lagging behind could make out the gentle engine noise—like bones grinding against one another—just behind the corner. Ignoring the existence of the building in front of it, a Legion fired its 120 mm cannon at them.

When faced with a shell capable of shattering a two-hundred-millimeter-thick steel plate, a stone wall was as effective as papier-mâché in the way of defense. It shattered like cracked glass at the impact, with the blast killing the straggling soldiers, and the debris of the stone wall ricocheting and cutting the surrounding soldiers to pieces, armor and all.

"Captaaaaaaain!"

"Stop—don't go back! There's no saving him anymore!"

A tank turret appeared from behind the toppled stone wall. Covered in heat haze, the Löwe's massive steel-colored frame swerved in their direction, its multiple legs not even regarding the mountain of rubble filling the street. There was no time to flee anymore. The Löwe confidently turned its muzzle toward the soldiers, who were left with only the freedom to glare at the opponent that would snuff out their lives...

There was the sound of heavy metal stabbing the pavement as it rushed in their direction. And then there was the sound of flagstones being cracked as something leaped into the air, whipping up a gale due to its immense speed.

A white shadow soared over the armored infantry's heads.

Landing on the wall of an apartment building on the left of the street and using it as a foothold, the white mech soared through the air, readjusting its direction in midleap. The Löwe failed to keep up with its opponent's irregular maneuvering, lifting its turret upward like a horse rearing up before the top of its armor was shot through.

Penetration. Internal explosion.

Blown up by its own ammunition's induced explosion, the Löwe burst into flames as its armor module flew off. The white-armored Feldreß landed before the soldiers' eyes, shielding them from the shock waves and the heat of the blast.

That white armor. That four-legged silhouette reminiscent of a decapitated skeletal corpse. And the Personal Mark of a headless skeleton carrying a shovel drawn beneath its canopy.

"A Regin...leif..."

The Reginleif's red optical sensor turned toward them.

"Are there any other squads out here?"

The infantry squad's vice captain noticed the white forms of several machines standing on the flat roofs of the apartments on both sides of the street. And the loud, clattering footsteps from behind the building couldn't have been the Legion's, who were equipped with powerful shock absorbers. They were lighter than a Vánagandr's, so there were probably more Reginleifs like this one deployed around them.

Finally noticing he was the one being asked here, the vice captain replied in a flustered manner. Depending on how many soldiers remained on the battlefield, if any, the strategies they could adopt were different. Even if they failed their duties and were forced to fall back, the least they could do was provide the allies who came to save them with what information they could.

"No one's left—we're the last ones! The other squads were all...all killed by those damned metal monsters."

"Right."

That reply came in a blunt, simple voice bereft of concern or grief. The Personal Mark of the rumored Reaper was that of a headless skeleton, meaning the one speaking to them now was...an Eighty-Six.

"Fall back and regroup. We'll buy you the time you need."

"All right, then. Let's begin."

Having been only recently deployed for test purposes, the XM2 Reginleif or "Juggernaut" was a Feldreß with a mobility that was unheard of in the Federacy's development history. In order to capitalize on its speed, it allowed for the changing of its weaponry—such as its main battery and grappling arms—for optional weapons depending on the strategy selected.

Anju's Snow Witch did away with the traditional 88 mm main bore gun, exchanging it for a multiple-launch rocket pad, making it a unit meant for area suppression. She'd heard the Legion's deployment positions from Shin before they launched into battle, and even though some time had passed, and they had moved significantly far from their positions at the time, she could imagine how they would move.

The ability to predict the enemy forces' position and hit that group for the maximum possible damage with one blow. That was the weapon Anju had cultivated over four years of deadly battle with the Legion and was the reason she'd survived to this day.

She inputted the enemy coordinates into the support computer and pulled the trigger. The missiles left a trail of smoke behind, and they each flew in different trajectories to minimize the risk of being intercepted, eventually reaching their designated targets.

The shells' fuses ignited, and the missiles scattered their smaller bombs. The Legion scattered as if in a panic, assailed by a rain of explosives.

Her tone was sweet, and she broke into a serene smile. But no one could know how terribly cruel Anju's smile was when she was alone in the cockpit.

"There they are. Scurrying around like ants after someone kicked their nest."

She observed the movements of the Legion moving across the ruins, through the head-mounted display she had on for precision aiming. They dispersed in a wide formation, cautious of the missiles' smaller bombs.

Kurena sat within Gunslinger, which was hidden in an old-fashioned church's belfry, setting her sights on one of the Legion. Gunslinger, which was specified for sniping, was equipped with a long-barreled 88 mm cannon designed to optimize ballistic stability and velocity. Its firearm-control and posture-control systems were also customized accordingly. All of that, coupled with Kurena's own talent for predictive sniping even in the face of the Legion's swift movements, left the research division struck with admiration for her accuracy ratio.

The head-mounted display projected data like wind velocity and temperature, as well as a cross-shaped reticle. Kurena squinted, listening to the sound of the Legion's wails coming from the Sensory Resonance. She didn't find these screams of suffering to be terrifying, and so long as these weren't the Black Sheep of her dead comrades, she didn't feel pity for them like Shin did.

To Kurena, the Legion were nothing more than a dangerous enemy that threatened her precious comrades—that threatened Shin, who led them across the battlefield.

And all enemies...

...must be eliminated.

As she held her breath, Kurena's golden eyes grew mercilessly cold. And naturally, almost casually, she squeezed the trigger, her bullet piercing and annihilating a Löwe in the distance.

"I took out their commanding unit. Changing position. Cover me."

"Roger that, Kurena! Leave these scrubs to me!"

Raiden's Wehrwolf had heavy machine guns in its grappling arms and had its main armament switched for an autocannon. Suppressive fire—a role that used barrages to halt the enemy's advance and support his consorts' advance.

After fighting alongside Shin—a vanguard who excelled at close-quarters combat—for three years, Raiden inevitably found himself in this role, which required adopting this kind of equipment and tactics. And at the same time, a role that amounted to supporting the rest of his unit was perfectly suited for a kind busybody like Raiden, who always kept an eye out for his comrades' well-being.

Not that he would ever admit that.

Each of the heavy machine guns and the autocannon were capable of locking on and firing at different targets. The heavy machine guns' dense barrage reduced the Ameise and Grauwolf who attempted to advance on him to scrap, and the autocannon's hail of bullets pinned down a team of two Löwe.

Two Juggernauts rushed in from Wehrwolf's sides. Undertaker cut down one of the Löwe as it passed beside it. Laughing Fox leaped up and bombarded the other one from above. Undertaker then rushed in and disappeared down a nearby street, while Laughing Fox launched a wire anchor to the top of a building and reeled itself up, heading down another street.

Kurena would provide cover fire for Shin. Anju had descended from the rear guard and was in the middle of reloading her missile launcher. Promptly analyzing the situation, Raiden decided to cover for Laughing Fox and changed Wehrwolf's bearing.

Theo's Juggernaut—Laughing Fox—was left as is with the standard configuration. He had an 88 mm smooth-bore gun, a heavy machine gun on one grappling arm, four pile drivers, and two wire anchors.

But his unique strategy was anything but standard.

"Up we go!"

Evading a Löwe's shot, Laughing Fox used an abandoned automobile as footing to jump up and fired an anchor into a building wall in midair, reeling it back to climb even higher. As the Grauwolf tried to scale up the wall to get to him, he mockingly shot an anchor into the building opposite them while releasing the first anchor. Reeling the anchor back, he zipped away, soaring directly above and behind the Löwe, pulling the trigger as he did. Taking an accurate shot right through its weak spot—the top rear section of its armor—the Löwe exploded.

Laughing Fox utilized wire anchors to achieve three-dimensional maneuvering. Even despite having to fight with a meager 57 mm cannon in the Republic's abandoned land, the Eighty-Six made urban fighting their expertise. And they were often pitted against Löwe and Dinosauria—whose only weak point required firing on them from above. These conditions, coupled with Theo's superior spatial perception, led him to this optimal answer. He knew he didn't have Shin's grappling skills to fight against the Legion in close-quarters combat and survive.

A lock-on alert blared.

Detecting that a Grauwolf had scaled the building up to the roof and aimed its rocket launcher in his direction from the corner of his eye, Theo fired another anchor. It latched onto another wall several buildings away. Using the anchor to run across the wall, he changed the bearing just as the explosion rang behind him, firing his machine gun at the Grauwolf and silencing it.

But in that moment, the fleeting glimpse he caught of the city below wiped the smile off his face.

In the front rows of the Nordlicht squadron's combat, the blur of a single pearly white Juggernaut was beset on all sides by the Legion flocking toward it. Shin truly was loved by the Reaper. Or maybe he really was the Reaper himself.

"God dammit… How can Shin keep pulling off these crazy-ass stunts and still manage to stay alive…?"

As those on the front lines risked life and limb, the personnel in the rear fought their own war.

"—Use every shell and energy pack we have! Roll out every truck that's ready!"

"Sergeant, the spare units are ready!"

"Have them ready to launch for whenever we get a request! C'mon, boys, don't rely on Fido! He's focused on supporting the captain and his team! It's our job to deliver these pizzas, you hear?!"

Having to worry about running out of ammo or energy while fighting the massive Legion would only make the soldiers on the front line that much closer to death. Those in the rear knew that a constant stream of supplies was the greatest form of reinforcements they could give right now and worked all the more diligently for it.

Realizing she would be heard better if there wasn't any noise around them, Frederica listened in on the goings-on in the hangar through the Para-RAID in her room in the barracks. Sitting with the RAID Device turned on, the girl restrained her emotions, which beckoned her to break into a run and do something. Her emotions screamed, telling her there had to be something, anything she could do to help. But she realized those thoughts only stemmed from self-satisfaction and suppressed her feelings with common sense.

In the hangar, heavy machinery zipped to and fro, carrying weighted energy packs and shells. The control room had Grethe and her crew of command specialists, who kept the situation under control with expert knowledge Frederica had no access to.

The least she could do was open her *eyes* and seek out her knight's whereabouts. Shin was fighting on the battlefield and likely didn't have the leisure to be occupied with Kiriya alone. But if he was to know his position, his actions, if she could even so much as warn him…

But when her *eyes* saw her knight, saw the battlefield he was on, the girl froze.

She fumbled over her RAID Device, hurriedly changing its target data. She urgently called out his name, half-dumbfounded.

"Shinei."

No response.

Shin was connected to the Resonance, though. As proof, she could hear the boisterous moans of the ghosts one would constantly hear when Resonating with Shin. She could hear his voice giving coolheaded orders even in the midst of frenzied battle. To his fellow Eighty-Six, to the Nordlicht squadron's other Processors, sometimes even using the wireless and his external speakers to talk to soldiers from other squadrons. He himself was probably running through enemy lines, cutting down countless foes as he did.

"Shinei… Kiri is absent."

No response.

Not wanting to believe he didn't hear her, she found herself repeating those words.

"Kiri is absent from the battlefield."

No response.

Frederica felt all the blood rush to her head. Not out of anger…but out of unfamiliar terror.

"Can you not hear me, Shinei?! Kiri is currently—"

At that moment, the target of her *eyes* changed to the person she was thinking of right then, the one she called out to again and again. She could see a four-legged spider rushing through city ruins in the dark of night. Its white fuselage had lost its pearly sheen. Dirtied in uneven strokes of silver and metallic gray by gunpowder smoke, dust, and spurts of liquid micromachines—the blood of the Legion he slew—the machine's color was corrupted.

A sight she had seen once before flashed in her mind's eye. A Feldreß splashed with the red of slaughtered soldiers, and next to it a person smiling pleasantly—with their black eyes frozen solid.

Princess.

And even as he spoke to her, those cold eyes never once looked at her. And the two red eyes she could see within that white armor had the same gaze.

He forcefully drove his blade, which had already lost its capacity to vibrate, into the enemy, rushing to face his next foe without even regarding the fact that it had shattered. His gaze didn't waver even as a shell's short-range fuse burst, sending debris tearing into his cockpit and smashing one of his sub-screens. He directed all his consciousness into the enemy before him and nothing more, his red eyes frozen sharply.

Frederica finally realized why he reminded her so much of Kiri.

It wasn't a matter of resemblance. They were the same. The two of them resembled each other so much because they were identical to their core.

You fool. The words spilled from her mouth noiselessly.

You are such a fool, Shinei. Even you do not understand.

Please stop.

"You mustn't fight when you get like this…!"

†

A crescent moon shone behind the thin silvery clouds, casting a gray-white shadow over the dim night ruins. Shin paused his heavy gait, holding his

breath in an attempt to listen and confirm the Legion's distribution status. He had since shut down his Juggernaut's radar, as it was useless at identifying friend from foe under the Eintagsfliege's closed skies.

"Whoa there, don't shoot, Nordlicht! I'm on your side!"

Farther along the way was a Vánagandr bearing the insignia of the 177th Armored Division's 56th Regiment. The Vánagandr's red optical sensor, set to tracking mode, turned toward Undertaker, and despite its weight of fifty tons, it approached him with light steps. Its suspension system hadn't been strained by battle yet.

...It seemed that the armored forces woken up by the siren were finally beginning to join the fight.

"That headless skeleton Personal Mark. You're the captain, right?"

"Second Lieutenant Shinei Nouzen, captain of the Nordlicht squadron... What's the situation?"

The Vánagandr's commander laughed, it seemed.

"Squad 56's captain, First Lieutenant Samuel Ruth. We managed to beat back the Legion's first wave, somehow. Same for the other sectors. It's all thanks to you scrambling as fast as you did. You all did real good."

What Shin wanted to hear was the status of their allies. He could already sense that the first wave of Legion had begun retreating from all fronts, but that wasn't worth mentioning. He'd rather this captain say something that helped him catch his breath after the battle.

"All the other units sortied already... It's all good now—you can fall back, get resupplied, and await further orders from HQ. From here on out, it's the Federacy's battle."

Don't force yourselves and retreat already, Eighty-Six.

Still trying to catch his breath, Shin inhaled deeply and said as he exhaled:

"With all due respect, First Lieutenant..."

Confirming the amount of remaining ammunition Fido—who was

on standby nearby—still had, he called up a multipurpose window displaying the status of the adjacent Juggernauts.

…It wasn't perfect, but it would do just fine. All the units were capable of continuing combat.

"…that battalion of Legion was only the advance force. The second wave is the main force… If we fall back now, this sector will fall."

All traces of laughter disappeared from the commander's voice.

"…What did you just say?"

"I leave defending this sector to you. We'll intercept the main force. If we take out the vanguards, it should slow down their advance a little."

"Wait, Second Lieutenant! What—?"

"Over and out— All units."

Cutting off the wireless communication one-sidedly, Shin called out to his comrades through the Para-RAID's Resonance. Sparing the frozen Vánagandr a final look, Undertaker turned its bearings toward the main force of the Legion—marching in the footsteps of its fallen advance force. Even from afar, the maelstrom of moans and laments threatened to deafen him.

Everyone's reply was immediate. Calming his disturbed breathing, he spoke plainly, with a trace of his occasional, savage smile.

"You heard everything. Follow me if you don't want to die."

†

The Legion's main force invaded, and the Federacy's armored forces arrived, forming a firm defensive line. The tidal wave of the Legion clashed against the solid defensive wall of the armored forces, locking them in a state of fluctuating stalemate. And it was when dawn rose, and the soldiers could finally see the hands gripping their guns, that someone noticed.

The morning light was red.

The soldiers who took cover in the trenches, who used collapsed buildings as barricades, who sat within the cramped cockpits of their Feldreß, looked up at the sky in between shots.

The sky was dyed crimson.

The light of dawn was reflected and refracted by the Eintagsfliege suffusing the heavens, blanketing the morning with a bloodred darkness, incurring the image of the world being sealed by flames. And beneath that red sky, the fighting continued.

The crimson light streamed through the countless piles of wreckage and mountains of corpses filling the ruins, casting horrific shadows, illuminating their outlines vividly as the fighting between mechanical monster and man raged on. And as they spouted blood and flames, more and more of them collapsed and created new shadows, becoming strokes of paint on the horrific canvas of red and black.

It was a vision of hell itself.

Some poor souls trapped in the black-red hell claimed to have seen a white nightmare. A pearly nightmare streaking across the battlefield, like a vivid hallucination. A headless skeleton, blessed with the name of a Valkyrie, that retained its ivory visage even among countless abrasions and dust.

They would stampede through key points, the collapse of which would spell an onslaught of Legion on many other sectors. They opposed the surging Legion's advance without allowing them to progress a single step by fighting like beasts tearing one another apart and inflicting precise, almost predicative bombardments.

They ignored any appeals for reinforcements or concerned voices from other squads that encouraged them to fall back. They had no forces to spare when fighting such a limitless army of Legion, and they probably knew that the Federacy's army would be crushed if they were to retreat. Or perhaps the idea of retreating was simply never a consideration for them, since they had spent years fighting with their backs to their homeland's minefield.

The wreckage of destroyed Legion units only piled up higher and higher, and they fought on, using it as cover. But as they fought, their ammo would eventually run out. Their energy packs would be depleted.

The Reginleif, which took maneuverability to its utmost extreme, was lightweight and couldn't carry much ammunition. And when the supplies they carried from base began running out, they stole the ammo of downed consort units. The obedient mechanical corpse collector that served as their attendant rummaged through the corpses of the deceased for them, piling up mechanical entrails on the wayside as it did.

The Vargus who lived in the old combat territories—the Wolfsland—during the Empire's rule and made the battlefield their home looked on at the Reginleifs' fighting style with awe. They smirked even in the middle of mortal combat, filled with joy and relief at the sight of their reliable comrades.

But most of the Federacy's soldiers saw it very differently. Namely, those sitting in the command tank, who had received the optical feed via data link. The armored infantry. The officers who served as Operators and their superiors all looked at the battle with abject shock.

"The Eighty-Six... They're...!"

These were their young comrades, who were reduced to pigs in human form by their homeland and cast out into the battlefield by the Republic. They thought them to be pitiable children. Deprived of their rights, stripped of their freedom, robbed of their families, their hometowns, and even their names. They were sent to the battlefield before they even had the chance to mature and were ordered to die a futile death at the end of their desperate struggles.

That's why everyone wished that, if nothing else, they could find happiness in the Federacy. And these children cut down that wish by their own hands.

They returned to the battlefield of their own will and plunged into even more lethal battle right now, before their eyes. They should not have had a reason to fight, no homeland or family to protect, no ideal to cling to. And in practice, they weren't defending anything. They ignored the voices of allied troops who sought aid and cannibalized the corpses of dead comrades to continue fighting. As if they longed for nothing but war, battle without reason or meaning.

They weren't innocent children, wounded by persecution. The

soldiers could see them only as monsters. Machines of slaughter, bred in the Republic's crucible of hatred and violence. Demons of war that rejected all salvation and compassion, born as man and twisted into beast through no fault of their own. Their warped hearts were beyond saving.

"They're monsters…!"

And despite the fact that the Eighty-Six themselves could have very well heard that hoarse whisper breathed into the wireless, no one remained to condemn whoever uttered it.

†

A short while ago, the reserve reaction unit's large transport touched down near FOB 15, and the armored units and mechanized infantry units aboard it hurried to the battlefield. Blue blips appeared, symbolizing that their allied units had significantly increased. Grethe was watching as the red and blue blips mingled together on the main screen, changing positions like a mosaic, when suddenly she noticed a new movement in the red camp.

The hodgepodge of red and blue parted.

Like grains of sand in an hourglass, the red color began spilling west, back to the territories under their control.

"The Legion are…"

All sensation of time had long since abandoned him. The surroundings reflected in his optical screen were dyed red, and he had lost count of how many enemies he destroyed and how many remained. He bit into solid combat rations in the pause between one battle and the next and closed his eyes for brief spells of rest. The Legion surged forth without schemes or tactics, making it not a battle but a primeval clash. He'd just barely managed to tell friend from foe, but if the battle lasted much longer, he couldn't say for sure that he would be able to continue making the distinction.

Raising his eyes, Shin suddenly realized it was raining. The Juggernaut's audio sensors picked up white noise and the sound of the faint rain pattering against its armor. It was the sound of peaceful silence, a rare occurrence on the tumultuous battlefield. And it took his exhausted consciousness a few seconds too long to realize why he could hear it.

The Legion were retreating. The voices of suffering were ebbing and growing fainter, and only the sounds of the Skorpion types' covering fire and the pursuit party's fighting echoed intermittently.

Opening his canopy, which felt as if it had been sealed forever, Shin exposed his body to the dreary rain and took a deep breath. The rain clouds parted, revealing a northern summer's faint sunset.

"All units."

His voice was a bit hoarse. He'd become acutely aware of the dryness in his throat. There were fewer responses compared to when they launched. Some of them probably didn't have the breath to raise their voice, and others may have not felt the need to respond... And some had probably lost the ability to reply, forever.

"All Legion forces have begun their retreat. Return to base."

When Undertaker touched down in the hangar's aircraft parking apron, Frederica awaited him there. Perhaps she hadn't slept, because the brims of her eyes were red. Her long hair, usually lovingly kept and combed by someone, was terribly frayed, too. Shin wondered whether she'd been waiting for him since he'd launched.

When their eyes met, Frederica's face contorted in sorrow. Her eyes filled with tears in what was a mix of relief and an equal measure of devastation. She embraced him as if she was incapable of restraining herself any longer.

"Shinei, you hopeless, irredeemable fool."

He didn't understand but extended his hand unconsciously, placing it on her tiny head. It was unusually free of her military cap. When he stroked her frayed black hair lightly, her delicate hands clung to him ever tighter.

"You are the same as Kiri... You complete and utter fool."

†

With the reserve units remaining vigilant in case of a repeated Legion attack, the western front's commanding officers still had their work cut out for them. They would need to replace and prepare the massive amounts of lost equipment and man power this battle cost them, send back the wounded and the deceased, repair damaged defensive facilities, analyze the battle...and confer honors.

The commanding officers all agreed that the greatest praise had to go to the controller in charge of the probe that had detected the Legion's advance long before anyone else did and had instructed other sectors to increase their range to specific values, consequently saving the western front from collapse.

However, that controller objected to the honors, claiming it wasn't he who'd scoped out the range in question. An officer had arrived, insisting he increase his vigilance over that area at all costs. He'd detected the Legion's advance force and sent the other sectors that instruction only because of that officer's persuasion.

"The controller put it in very reasonable terms, but in practice, you employed some rather forceful measures, Second Lieutenant Shinei Nouzen."

The general's office remained furnished pretty much as it had been during the Empire's time. The major general spoke, seated behind a dignified mahogany desk, with service ribbons lined up on his uniform, a cross-shaped medal on his collar, and a black eyepatch covering his missing eye.

"A Federacy soldier always keeps his gun trained on his enemies but never uses it to threaten and coerce his allies. Even if he never did actually point the muzzle at them."

"...I thought the credit for detecting the enemy would be a proper apology. He'd have been promoted for sure if he'd just kept his mouth shut and taken it."

The major general narrowed his eye in scrutiny at that indifferent answer, and Greta, who stood at the back, cradled her forehead in her hand. As he stood between them in an at-ease pose, Shin's expression remained still.

It would only be natural that he would be tried and punished for his repeated arbitrary uses of his authority and breaches of regulation, even if they were necessary. He was actually sure he'd be arrested given what he'd done to the controller, but for the time being, he was only being questioned, probably because they were still unsure as to how to treat him.

Swerving his leather chair to look away from him, the major general regarded a tablet terminal before raising his lone eye.

"You've said some very interesting things in your hearing with the military police… Something about you being able to hear the Legion's voices, and that's how you could tell where they were."

Grethe cut into the conversation, unable to keep quiet any longer.

"Major General. I know it's hard to believe, but it's true. Troops that Resonated their hearing with Second Lieutenant Nouzen's using the RAID Device have given reports that endorse his claims…"

"I don't recall giving you permission to speak, Lieutenant Colonel. I already know that people with such abilities exist. I've read the reports, as well. But those don't serve as solid enough proof at this point."

He punched a few commands into the information terminal in his hand, and a map of the battlefield appeared over the desk. His black eye locked on Shin from beyond the holographic map.

"Tell me where they are. Mark the ten closest spots on the map."

Sneaking a glance aside, Shin detected a camouflaged surveillance camera on the ceiling and an intercom hidden between the tablet and a sheet of paper. It seemed their idea was to cross-reference real-time information with their radar transmissions to confirm his words. *Whatever the method itself is, it's certainly the most direct way of checking if I'm saying the truth*, Shin thought as he sighed to himself.

"…Pardon me."

He sought the position of the closest unit he could sense and marked it on the map, and then he marked the ten closest units in comparison to it. He could pick up the Legion's distance and direction accurately, but not in accordance to standard units of distance. It was one thing in the Republic's familiar zones, but this map was of the division's zones, which were far larger. It was harder to tell the exact distance. When Shin marked the seventh point, the major general's eye narrowed. He said something through the intercom—apparently, Shin had detected a Legion force they weren't aware of.

When Shin finished giving his response, the major general gave a long, deep sigh.

"…There's one thing I have to ask you."

Pausing to think, he opened his mouth.

"Why did you choose this method, boy? Even if it saved the western front, your actions very much jeopardized your position. You had to have known this. Why put yourself in danger like that?"

"I concluded that if I'd gone through standard procedure, I wouldn't have made it in time to impede the attack… And besides, if I had told you this before, you wouldn't have believed me."

"That's not an answer. I'm asking why you didn't consider your own well-being… You're an Eighty-Six. Surely you'd think we could have treated you as an alerting mechanism or a guinea pig."

The Eighty-Six were already treated as pigs in human form by their homeland, after all.

"Yes… But if I didn't, we'd have lost to the Legion, and all would have been for naught."

The major general fell silent for a long moment.

"I see. So you would put yourself at any risk if it meant you could slaughter your enemy. That's your…the Eighty-Six's answer. Truly, you are like a blade. You would resolve to be cut down, even if it meant you shattered in the aftermath."

Silencing Grethe, who was about to burst into words again, the major general said:

"I will overlook the matter, this time… Can I expect you to report it the next time you sense a similar threat?"

"Yes."

"Lieutenant Colonel, you are to receive his reports in such an occasion. Report them to me through a direct line. I allow it. I'll let my aide know."

*   *   *

As soon as they left the general's office, Grethe opened her mouth to speak with a sigh.

"Please stop scaring me like that, Second Lieutenant. The subject in question was one thing, but that was no way to talk to a commanding officer."

"I'm sorry."

"Good grief... And for the love of God, do try to consider your own safety. It will only lead to you keeping those around you safe...First Lieutenant Nouzen."

Grethe shrugged at Shin's inquisitive stare.

"Everyone in the squadron who was a higher rank than you died. It happens a lot in the Federacy's army."

She smirked bitterly, remembering how that very same process granted her the lieutenant colonel rank insignia shining on her collar now, despite her being in her midtwenties.

"And you were the de facto squad captain, so it's perfectly appropriate... I actually wanted to promote you one rank higher, but this debacle ended up offsetting that."

"..."

"You could look a bit happier or disappointed, you know. If nothing else, your salary is going to increase. Not that it makes much of a difference to you."

His necessary expenses were deducted from his salary as it was, and he never used it for anything else, so he probably didn't think much of it either way.

"I swear... That's all I had to say. Dismissed, First Lieutenant."

"...I'll take my leave, then."

Parting with Grethe, who returned to her office, Shin walked down the carpeted hallway and sighed in his mind, wondering what to do going forward. The western front had taken severe damage in the battle, and there wasn't much left for them to do now that the reserves had taken over defending the area while the army reorganized itself.

For starters, he decided to confirm his comrades' status, which he hadn't been able to infer during his several days of questioning, and turned to go back to the Nordlicht squadron's barracks, which were once again in their home base. Just as he was about to go, he noticed the patter of light footsteps approaching him.

Lifting his gaze, he saw it was Frederica. The soles of her hard army boots trampled the carpet, and she approached him with a desperate demeanor that didn't fit the base's current calm-after-the-storm atmosphere.

It was then that he felt the presence of a gaze fixed on them from afar. Black eyes frozen in hatred and loathing.

"—I´ll kill them all."

A chill ran down his spine.

How, how could he have forgotten?

He'd encountered it twice already and knew it was the Legion's trump card. And despite that, he'd unconsciously stopped considering it to be a threat. And that was because somewhere in his heart he believed that even if *it* were to destroy a fortress far in the battlefield, or a country, or even humankind itself, it wouldn't truly influence him. That was true for him and for the Eighty-Six who made the battlefield their homeland. Those who had only the death of the enemy before them or their own death as their fate...

But the truth was, they never did escape the battlefield of the Eighty-Sixth Sector. He realized that now.

"Get down!" shouted Frederica. "Kiri is—"

Those words overlapped with the screech of a high-speed projectile tearing through the atmosphere and the earth-shattering shock waves of an extremely heavy mass's impact. A flash of blinding light glinted outside the window, painting the world white.

Ear-ripping reverberations that were so powerful they almost sounded like silence ripped through the air like the rumbling of thunder. The following shock waves shook the fortress down to its very foundations.

WHEN "JOHN DOE" COMES MARCHING HOME

"The northern front's first ward's first defensive squadron Sledgehammer to all Eighty-Six... All Processors hearing this broadcast."

His partner was lying demolished nearby, its main armament and armor crushed brutally by a kick delivered by a fifty-ton Löwe. It would never move again. He himself crawled out of the wreckage, dragging his injured right lower half as he made his way to an old bridge on the edge of the battlefield. Reclining against the stone guardrail was the most he could manage, and keeping his eyes open was agony. The blood smeared over the bleached armor of his machine and dripping from his lower half was a dark shade of red, noticeable even in the darkness of night.

"This is the Sledgehammer squadron's captain, Black Bird."

His squadmates had all died in battle by now, and he didn't know whether any other squadrons in the ward were even still alive. They truly had been beaten, hands down.

The Legion boasted high power and fidelity the Juggernaut could normally never hope to match. And a massive army of them, the size of which they'd never encountered before, had suddenly invaded. A small force like them hadn't stood a chance. And despite that, they'd still sortied. Even though what stood at their backs was neither a homeland they were to defend nor a family to return to. And they fought on despite that.

"Our war is over."

Because that was the last pride they—the Eighty-Six—had left.

A single Löwe drew close to him, the moonlight reflecting off its frosted armor as it carried its heavy, metallic body with near inaudible footsteps. It probably couldn't be bothered to waste a shell to kill this mouse it had cornered, as it didn't even aim its 12.7 mm heavy machine guns or its menacing 120 mm turret at him. It drew on him with the composed confidence of a predator, its massive frame occupying the full width of the bridge.

Looking up at the metal menace looming over him, Black Bird smirked thinly. He knew, somehow, there were fellow Eighty-Six out there listening to the words he spoke into the wireless, set to a one-directional transmission.

"All Processors listening to this. All those who fought to the bitter end. All those who survived. We're finally discharged. We all...did a great job."

Here in this battlefield of zero casualties, where there was no salvation or recompense, and the only thing that waited was an uncompromising death.

Having said all he had to say, Black Bird switched off the transmission and threw away his headset. He took the small remote control his crushed right hand had still grasped, holding it up in his left. The Löwe drew closer, standing right before him on the bridge as he powerlessly leaned back.

Five years ago, he met the captain of the first squadron he was assigned to. He was a soldier in the Republic's old ground forces and an Eighty-Six banished to the battlefield. And he taught him how to fight, how to survive, and how to use this thing. And there sure as hell wasn't anyone among the white pigs who would be capable or willing to pull this stunt off.

Despite his hideously burned lips and cut skin, he smiled almost cheerfully. He wouldn't give up on living without yielding to despair, and he wouldn't let hatred taint his dignity, either. He'd fought all the way here, having chosen to live as such.

But he was allowed to say this much in the end, right? Looking up at the metallic limb swung over him like a scythe, he pressed the SELF-DESTRUCT switch with a smile.

You pathetic, wretched white pigs of the Republic who forced your war on others, shut your eyes from reality, and in so doing lost all means to defend yourselves. You who forfeited the right to choose your own deaths...

"—Serves you right."

The plastic explosive planted on the bridge girder detonated. On this old bridge, which served as the river crossing's key position, one metallic tyrant of the land was consumed by flames and tumbled into the river, accompanied by one tenacious Eighty-Six who wouldn't even be counted among the dead.

Year 368 of the Republic calendar, August 25, 23:17.

When the alarm rang in the military's headquarters, not a soul present knew what it meant. It was understandable, in a way, as it had been configured ten years ago. It was the members of the ground forces, who'd defended the nation before them and been decimated down to their rear personnel, who'd set that siren with the resolve and hope that it would never have to be heard.

The large holo-screen set for briefing purposes switched on automatically. The holographic screen, set over most of the wall, projected distorted footage corrupted by the darkness of the night and electronic jamming. As her colleagues gazed at the monitor with annoyance and grumbling, Lena alone swallowed in vague terror as she looked up at the footage.

The footage showed the ruins of a structure built in the shape of a wall, shattered from top to bottom, its destroyed concrete and armor plates large enough to cover a small house each. Due to the structure's size, the scars of its destruction were as massive as a ravine. And crossing over that ravine like a metal-colored stream was a massive army of multilegged machines built to maximize their potential for slaughter.

Lena felt a shudder of horror rush up her spine.

"What is this, a movie? Looks cool."

"Someone turn off that siren; it's annoying."

She took a staggered step back, distancing herself from her colleagues, who wallowed in blissful ignorance because they were not aware of the crippling fear that *they* could inspire. The Republic had shut itself in, pushing the war onto the Eighty-Six for a decade now. The grand majority of its civilians—even its military personnel—had no knowledge of what their enemy even looked like. Lena was the exception, because she had seen them before.

Six years ago, when she was taken to see the front lines—when she lost her father, and Rei saved her. And another time, when she Resonated her eyesight with Raiden's to provide covering fire for the Spearhead squadron.

The ones leading the stream, with an angular shape reminiscent of a man-eating fish, were the Scout-type Ameise. The ones with six legs, which granted them exceptional maneuverability and allowed them to hop over the collapsed walls with ease, were the Dragoon-type Grauwolf. The ones crossing through in an orderly line, their 120 mm tank turrets swerving in all four directions, were the Tank-type Löwe. And finally, the ones who crushed the rubble beneath their massive weight, rushing through the uninhabited fields like haughty tyrants, were the Heavy Tank–type Dinosauria.

And the collapsed structure, constructed with only absolute, impenetrable defense in mind…was the Gran Mur.

This siren…was to alert the fall of the final defensive line.

"……!"

The time was finally upon them.

The Legion had built up their forces, cloaked by the Eintagsfliege's jamming, and today was the day when they would go on the offensive.

The day when the Republic would collapse under the weight of its hubris, having shielded its eyes from reality and chosen to live in a fragile dream of fabricated peace. Just as Shin once warned her.

A multitude of Legion crossed the collapsed Gran Mur in swarms, in hordes, in droves, with nothing standing in their way to the eighty-five Sectors... To the Republic of San Magnolia, which had forgotten how to defend itself in its dream of eternal peace. The majority of them were probably Black Sheep, Legion that had taken in human neural networks to conquer their set life spans. An army of the ghosts of the hundreds of thousands of Eighty-Six the Republic had cast out and used up on the battlefield.

That army of ghosts had finally made its return.

Something flashed on the black horizon beyond the ruins of the fortress walls and the tidal wave of steel, like a will-o'-the-wisp meant to lure men into a bottomless marsh. That awn-like blue light was the glare of an optical sensor. Its silhouette wavered in the moonlight, perspective warping its massive size—a colossal shadow, as large as a building or some gigantic monster of myth.

It lifted its front half up in a hulking fashion, and for some reason, the noise distorting the footage became more severe. It was then that she suddenly realized. This disastrous sight of the Gran Mur, which looked as if it had been repeatedly beaten and crushed by this titan... As if it had been destroyed by *bombardment*.

A flash filled the screen, and the footage was lost.

The holo-screen turned eerily black instantaneously. The camera... The place where it was set was probably blown away. The siren screeched without end.

It was the same as that time. The Spearhead squadron encountered something like this once before on the first ward's battlefield, forcing even elites like them into retreat. A high-speed, high-range shower of shells that exceeded the range of what should have been possible for artillery. The new Long-Range Artillery type.

"...Railgun."

Lena whispered, pursing her lips.

Lena turned on her heels resolutely, leaving behind the office and her colleagues, who kept on yammering without any sense of impending crisis, dubious at best. Her military boots clicked against the wooden corridor's floor as she made her way to her control room.

Her RAID Device singed with illusory heat, and she activated her Sensory Resonance. She had received two concurrent calls—one from one of the wings of the research division and another from one of the Queen's Knights in a faraway combat sector.

"Lena! That siren just now...!"

"Letting you know just in case, Your Majesty! The northern front...!"

"Yes, Annette. And I'm aware of the situation, Cyclops. They've finally come."

She changed her RAID Device's setting, allowing her to Resonate with all possible targets in range. Normally, a Handler would be allowed to Resonate with only one squadron, but Annette had cooperated with her over the past year to set up this hidden setting.

An army of ghosts of countless Eighty-Six the Republic had cast out and used up on the battlefield. If they were to fight back against it, they would need to consolidate all their forces. To fight back. To live on and answer the words *they* left behind.

"Bloody Reina to all Processors on all fronts!"

The Federacy military officially dubbed it the Railgun type. This new type of Legion single-handedly toppled the Gran Mur and burned the Federacy's fortress base to cinders. It was what appeared on the last observed footage discovered in the headquarters' ruins...

(To be continued...)

AFTERWORD

Pilot suits are nothing more than decoration! Hello, everyone, this is Asato Asato.

I've always been oddly fascinated with the question of "Why do pilot suits have to have full-body tights?" Of course, a lot of them have special features or settings, but do pilots suits really always have to be like that? Especially with robots that are used for ground combat, why don't the pilots wear tanker jackets like real tankmen?

No, I mean, I *do* get it. It's because girls in pilot suits are cute. And cute is righteous. But my book's protagonist, Shin, is a guy...! And that's why in *86—Eighty-Six*, I had them fighting in field uniforms. This volume has them in panzer jackets, though.

While revising Volume 1, I said, "If possible, I'd like to avoid pilot suits...," and halfway through Volume 2, I screamed "No pilot suits, aaaaaaah!" and thankfully, my kindhearted editor gave me the okay. Yay! But we did agree that "we want to see Lena in a pilot suit at some point." So fellow girls-in-pilot-suits enthusiasts should look forward to that, albeit patiently.

Not to worry—I stick to my beliefs. Cute is righteous. Girls in pilot suits are righteous!

Now, then.

So Volume 2! I continued the story! I continued it!! And it's all thanks to your fervent support, loyal readers! Thank you so much!! And my sincerest apologies for dropping a two-parter on you right off the bat. I intended for this to be only one volume, but I wanted to write everything I wanted to write, and as I put in more and more content, it got longer than I'd anticipated...

In terms of the content, this volume goes into the events and people mentioned in Volume 1's epilogue, making it a story about a faction with quite a lot of people in it. Also, while Volume 1 is told mostly from Lena's perspective, I had Volumes 2 and 3 focus more on Shin. This series's title is *Eighty-Six*, after all.

So why did I use this derogatory term used by the Republic even after they escaped the Republic's battlefield? What does *Eighty-Six* even mean? I intended for this his-and-hers story to be the curtain-raiser for the story that begins with this volume.

Some commentary for this time:

- The Juggernaut's main turret:

In this volume, the Juggernaut is equipped with an 88 mm cannon that is technically dubbed a Ratsch Bumm. But in the real world, the Ratsch Bumm was a nickname given to a Soviet 76 mm anti-tank gun. Why not just use an 88 mm cannon's nickname, you ask? I suggest you look up what the World War II German 8.8 cm Flak 36 antiaircraft gun was nicknamed and then check this book's jacket or cover.

...Get it? It's a classic example of how deciding your pen name without really thinking too deeply about it can land you in trouble later down the road.

- The title:

While we're on the topic of my pen name, I've been asked a few times about the origins of the title *Eighty-Six*. It comes from English slang, where to eighty-six someone means you designate them as someone who isn't allowed to enter a store or as someone you refuse to give service to. But it also carries the nuance of ejecting someone, disposing of them, or murdering them.

Lastly, some thanks.

To Kiyose and Tsuchiya, my editors who patiently stuck with me and gave me all the right advice as I was constantly straying off course while writing this rapidly changing manuscript.

To Shirabii, who decorated this brutal story with lovely illustrations. This volume's new female character appears a lot, and you made her quite brilliant!

To I-IV, who brought all my puzzling settings to life with this new strong Juggernaut. I look forward to seeing how you work on that one thing in Volume 3!

And to all of you who picked up this volume. I'm cranking out Volume 3 as we speak, so let's meet again in Volume 3, *Run Through the Battlefront (Finish)*!

In any case, I hope that for even a short moment, I was able to let you experience that journey to beyond where the sun rises, to the summer of that northern militant nation. To run by their side once again, on that battlefield of blood and iron.

Music playing while writing this afterword: "Run Through the Jungle" by Creedence Clearwater Revival